CLOVER TWIG
and
the PERilous Path

CLOVER TWIG and the PERilous Path

By
KAYE UMANSKY

Illustrated by
JOHANNA WRIGHT

SQUARE FISH

ROARING BROOK PRESS · NEW YORK

SQUARE
FISH

An Imprint of Macmillan
175 Fifth Avenue, New York, NY 10010
mackids.com

Square Fish books may be purchased for business or promotional use. For
information on bulk purchases, please contact the Macmillan Corporate and
Premium Sales Department at (800) 221-7945 x 5442 or by e-mail at
specialmarkets@macmillan.com.

Library of Congress Cataloging-in-Publication Data
Umansky, Kaye.
    Clover Twig and the perilous path / Kaye Umansky ; illustrated by Johanna
Wright.
        p. cm.
    Sequel to: Clover Twig and and the magical cottage.
    Summary: Clover Twig has been warned about The Perilous Path, but when her
baby brother goes missing she and her friend Wilf must travel that tricky trail to
rescue him from the clutches of Mesmeranza, the evil sister of Clover's employer,
Mrs. Eckles.
    ISBN 978-1-250-02727-6
[1. Witches—Fiction.   2. Household employees—Fiction.   3. Trails—
Fiction.   4. Missing children—Fiction.   5. Magic—Fiction.   6. Brothers and
sisters—Fiction.]   I. Title.
    PZ7.U363Cls 2012
    [Fic]—dc23
                                                                            2011031726

Originally published in the United States by Roaring Brook Press
First Square Fish Edition: June 2013
Square Fish logo designed by Filomena Tuosto

10 9 8 7 6 5 4 3 2 1

LEXILE: 570L

To Mo and Ella

CHAPTER ONE

She's Got a Visitor

It was Saturday morning, and Clover Twig was walking through the woods, on her way back from the village of Tingly Bottom. Her basket was heavy with all the things she needed for breakfast.

Mrs. Eckles always insisted on a thumping great fry-up on Saturdays, because on Fridays she stayed up all night doing the Protection Ritual—a long-winded business involving chalked diagrams, smelly potions, and endless dreary hours of mystic muttering. Clover had stayed up to watch her do it once but kept falling asleep out of boredom.

Clover didn't really like being involved in the magical side of things. Oh, *some* of it was interesting, but she had enough to do as it was. Keeping house for a Witch is hard work.

She had gotten up bright and early to make the trip, leaving Mrs. Eckles rattling the rafters with her snores. It had taken the best part of an hour to reach the village and another hour to get served by Old Trowzer— one half of the pair of Old Trowzers who ran the shop. He had a puffy purple face and moved maddeningly slowly, like a snail swimming in jelly. He talked slowly too. He made people twitch and want to finish his sentences for him.

Clover was the only customer, so he really took his time. He weighed each sausage separately. He dribbled milk into the can drop by precious drop. When Clover ordered a bag of strawberry drops, he spent ten minutes finding the jar, ten minutes getting it down, and another ten unscrewing the top. He dropped the sweets into the bag one by one while Clover tried not to fidget.

He inquired if business was good for Mrs. Eckles and tried to pry a bit, but Clover kept her answers short. She was glad to escape.

She was enjoying the walk back, though. Speckled sunlight filtered through the trees, the birds were singing, and everything smelled of summer. Best of all, tomorrow was her day off!

The trees thinned—and there it was. The cottage. Hunched and waiting in the middle of a small clearing. Staring at her with its dark windows in a *knowing* sort of way and letting off a ghostly trickle of black smoke from its twisty chimney, although the fire wasn't lit. Giving off a bad impression in general. Mrs. Eckles said that bad first impressions were important.

Hefting her basket, Clover walked up to the gate.

"Open up," she said.

"What, *again*?" snapped the gate, rudely. Clover made a mental note to give it a drop of oil. Not too much, or it got over-polite, which was worse.

"*Yes*, again. Quick, this is heavy."

"Open, shut, open, shut," grumbled the gate. "I'm sick of it."

"Look," said Clover, "you've got a choice. Oil later or a kick right now. Which will it be?"

Reluctantly, shedding rust, creaking, squeaking, and

generally making a great to-do, the gate edged open. She was just about to slip through when it said, sulkily, "She's got a visitor."

"She has? Who?"

Clover was surprised. Mrs. Eckles rarely had visitors apart from Wilf, who didn't count. There was the odd customer, of course. From time to time, nervous-looking locals would come sidling around to the back door, asking for a jar of ointment or a bottle of tonic or a tea-leaf reading. But today was Saturday. Mrs. Eckles never worked on Saturdays.

"Wouldn't *you* like to know?" sneered the gate. Clover ignored it and stepped through. She would find out soon enough.

The front yard looked much the same as the day she had first come to work for Mrs. Eckles, back in the spring. Clover was always trying to neaten it up. Forever sneaking out to hack back ivy and pull up weeds. She had even tried planting a tub with daffodils. But it was pointless. The daffodils wilted and the weeds always grew back.

She didn't bother with the front door, which was permanently sealed and just for show. Instead, she crunched up the path and went around the side, past the outhouse and the log pile to the backyard.

The backyard! My, what a contrast! Flowers bloomed and chickens scratched and the sun shone and birds sang in the cherry tree. Mrs. Eckles's voice rang out from the open door.

". . . Clover's 'er name. Jason Twig's daughter, the one who reckons he's got a bad back but spends all his time propping up the bar in the Crossed Axes. She does the cookin', keeps the place tidy. Good little worker. Uses 'er brains."

Clover stopped and listened. She couldn't help it. It's always interesting to hear about yourself.

"Dunno if you 'eard, but I had a bit o' trouble with my sister back in the spring. I was away at the time, at the May Fair over in Palsworthy. Did you go this year? No? Just as well, rained out, total disaster. Anyway, I left Clover to mind the cottage. Well, she seemed sensible. And I'd doubled up the security, told 'er the threshold rule about not invitin' anyone in, all that. Thought I 'ad everythin' covered. Never crossed my mind there'd be a problem . . ."

Mrs. Eckles broke off as Clover appeared in the doorway. She was sitting at the kitchen table opposite her visitor, still in her dressing gown, clearly not long out of bed.

The visitor was a vision in wintry gray. She had

iron-gray curls, chilly gray eyes, and a tight little mouth. Despite the warmth of the day, she was muffled up in a variety of gray shawls and thick overcoats. Atop her head was a pointy hat, also gray. A large, serious-looking handbag sat on her lap.

"Here she is!" cried Mrs. Eckles, clearly relieved. "Just who I was talkin' about! Clover, this is Mrs. Dismal, all the way over from Piffle."

Ah. Right. Granny Dismal, the Witch from the next village. Clover had never met her, but Mrs. Eckles had spoken of her in highly unflattering terms. *Pretends to be disinterested in anythin' you've got to say, but takes it all in, then uses it against you. Keen on magical technology. Don't get her going on that, she'll bore you rigid. Always orderin' the latest newfangled gadget from catalogues when everyone knows the old ways are best. Far-seein' telescopes, floatin' pens, all that rubbish. Collects Crystal Balls. Spends an unhealthy amount of time snoopin' on 'em, hopin' for a crossed line.* That sort of thing.

Mind you, it wasn't just Granny Dismal. Mrs. Eckles didn't have time for any of the Witches from the outly-ing villages, and it seemed that the feeling was mutual. Mrs. Eckles said that even the annual potluck dinner was an unfriendly event, where everyone brought potato salad and left early.

"Hello," said Clover, dropping her head in a polite little bob.

6

Granny Dismal said nothing. Her bleak eyes flickered briefly over Clover, then wandered past and fixed on a rafter.

"So you won't stay for a cup of tea, Ida?" inquired Mrs. Eckles, clearly hoping she wouldn't.

"No," said Granny Dismal in a voice like a wet day in February. "I'm all right."

"Of course, I was forgettin', you only drink your own special blend," said Mrs. Eckles, rather waspishly. "Out of yer special cup."

"That's right."

"You didn't bring it? The cup?"

"No. I'm not staying." Granny Dismal's expressionless eyes were moving slowly around the kitchen. You could tell she was taking it all in. Clover was glad she had left things tidy.

"Well then . . ." Mrs. Eckles scrambled to her feet, all ready and eager to show her out.

"I said I'd stay for ten minutes," said Granny Dismal. "There's three to go."

Mrs. Eckles sat down again. A heavy silence fell. The grandfather clocked ticked.

"Well," said Clover, taking pity. "I'll make *you* some, shall I, Mrs. Eckles?"

"There's a good girl!" cried Mrs. Eckles. "I'm that dry with all the conversation."

If she was being sarcastic, it was wasted on Granny Dismal. Clover busied herself with the kettle.

"Anyway, I was tellin' you about what 'appened back in spring . . ." began Mrs. Eckles.

"No need," said Granny Dismal. "I heard. Your sister tried to snatch the cottage. Mother Flummox told me."

"Oh. Right."

Clover poured milk. Behind her, the silence rolled out.

"So, did you get yourself that new Crystal Ball you was wantin'?" inquired Mrs. Eckles, desperately clutching at straws. "You was talkin' about it at the last pot-luck, before we all walked out. The one with—what was it? Extra pixie stations?"

"Pixilation," said Granny Dismal. For the first time, she showed a hint of animation. "The Ballmaster Multi-dimensional Mark Six with extra pixilation."

"Right. Good, is it?"

"State of the art. All automatic, no hand gestures required. Perfect picture, self-adjusting. Boldly goes where no Ball has gone before. Don't require a receiving Ball. Any reflecting surface will do."

"Mmm," said Mrs. Eckles. "I don't go in for Balls meself."

"I know. It's very inconvenient. Folks have to drag themselves around in the flesh."

8

"Well, I'm sorry, but I just don't trust 'em. All them pesterin' calls. Spyin' eyes. Crossed lines. Never know who's snoopin', do you? My sister's got one and I ain't riskin'—"

"She's smaller than I thought," interrupted Granny Dismal, suddenly. She spoke directly to Mrs. Eckles, as though Clover wasn't there. "The girl. Living in, you say?"

"Yep. Got a bed up in the attic."

"I wouldn't have that. Somebody living above. Coming in late, banging about."

"She don't come in late. She's a good girl."

"They are to *start* with. Then they start taking advantage. Acting cheeky."

Clover had had enough of this. She placed the milk jug on the table with a little more force than was necessary, and said, "I am *here* you know."

"You see?" said Granny Dismal, picking up her handbag and rising. "Just what I was talking about."

"Well, ta-ta then, Ida," said Mrs. Eckles, springing up and hurrying to the door. "The ten minutes is up, don't want to keep you. Oh—thanks for the warnin'."

"Someone's got to do it," said Granny Dismal, turning up her many coat collars and adjusting her various shawls. "I'll contact the rest by Ball."

Mrs. Eckles watched Granny Dismal waddle off around the side of the cottage. She seemed to move inside her own miserable weather system.

"Mind the gate!" shouted Mrs. Eckles. "It'll go for your fingers!" She shut the door, leaned against it with closed eyes, and said, "Give me strength!"

"How long has she been here?"

"Too bloomin' long. Thought she'd be in an' out, but she hung around waitin' to get a look at you."

"I don't know why," said Clover, rather crossly. "She just looked right through me." She spooned tea leaves into the pot and added, "So what was the warning?"

"Eh?"

"You said thanks for the warning. About what?"

"Ah, tell you later."

"Why not now?"

" 'Cause some tales don't go with sunshine an' sausages. Some tales are better told over the fire on nights when the cold wind's a-howlin' in the eaves."

"It's summer," Clover pointed out. "There won't *be* a howling wind."

"There will be if I want one," said Mrs. Eckles firmly. "Wind's easy. Did you get the sausages?"

"I did. The herbed ones, your favorite."

"Get the fryin' pan out, then. Ah, 'ere he comes!"

Mrs. Eckles's voice went all gooey. "'Ere's mother's baby . . . *ooh! Bad* boy!"

Neville the cat came leaping through the window with a bewildered baby bird clamped between his jaws. The next few minutes were filled with flying feathers; scolding, panicky chirps; and finally, happy airborne flappings, followed by feline sulks, eventual forgiveness, and bowls of milk. Then came the sound of sizzling sausages as Clover set about making breakfast. She sliced mushrooms and dropped eggs in the skillet while Mrs. Eckles slurped tea and talked about gardening.

After breakfast—a long, serious affair, accompanied by demands for extra mustard and more toast—Clover's real work started. There were dishes to be washed and the floor to mop and eggs to collect and logs to be carted and lamp wicks to trim and the gate to oil and all the other hundred and one jobs that always need doing when you are keeping house for a Witch.

The Witch herself showed no signs of doing anything much. Still in her dressing gown, she wandered out into the backyard, inspected the flowers, chatted to Flo and Doris, the chickens, filled the bird feeder in the cherry tree, sat on a bench, did a row of knitting, then snoozed in the sunshine.

* * ★ * *

Clover forgot all about her question until the evening. Supper was over and the fire was banked high because, funnily enough, a chilly wind was coming up. The curtains were drawn, the lamps glowed, and Mrs. Eckles was rambling on about running low on herbs and needing to go out picking sometime soon. She said the same thing most nights, and Clover was feeling sleepy and not really listening. Until two words made her open her eyes and sit up.

"What? What did you just say?"

"The Perilous Path, " said Mrs. Eckles. You could hear the capital letters. "It's back. That's what Ida came to warn about. Says she saw the glow over the trees through her telescope. Reckon I'll leave the pickin' for a few nights."

The fire spat, making Clover jump and shadows leap. The kitchen suddenly seemed darker. Outside, the wind moaned.

"I didn't know there was a Perilous Path," said Clover. "Where does it lead?" She thought she knew all the paths in the wood. Some were muddier than others, and some had nasty potholes or low branches that

clonked your head, but she knew Mrs. Eckles wasn't talking about those.

"Nowhere good." Mrs. Eckles's green eyes gleamed in the firelight. Far away, out in the dark woods, a lone wolf began howling.

"I think the wolf's a bit too much," said Clover.

"You do? All right, I'll tone it down." Mrs. Eckles twiddled her fingers and the howl cut off.

"Go on," said Clover. "About this Path. Have *you* been down it?"

"Not likely. I got more sense. Never 'eard the old saying? *Woe! Seven Times Woe Betide All Ye Who Walk the Perilous Path!*"

"Woe?" said Clover. "Why woe? What woe?" There was something about Mrs. Eckles's doomy tones and the wind and the wolf and everything that made her want to giggle. But in a slightly nervous way.

"Don't laugh," said Mrs. Eckles. "I'm serious. I'm talkin' about troubles an' dangers an' temptations an' all kinds o' time-wastin' malarkey you can do without. Your worst nightmares come true."

"I don't have nightmares."

"Everyone has nightmares. You've probably forgotten 'em."

The wind whistled in the chimney. Neville hissed in his sleep and flicked his tail.

14

"Who made the Path?" asked Clover.

"Nobody *made* it. It just—*is*."

"Have you seen it?"

"Come across it a few times."

"So, what's it like? Is it—*magical* looking?"

"Can be. Depends who it's tryin' to attract. It's crafty. Oh, it can put on a proper show when it wants. Kinda sparkles an' dazzles in an *allurin'* way. Some folks is easily dazzled. Or it can catch you off guard. Creeps up on you, disguised like a normal path."

"How d'you mean?"

"You know. Pathy. Dirt, bushes, trees, what else? Look, it's after sunset, right, and you're walkin' along some old track you've walked a hundred times before. Stoppin' to pick an herb or two. Everythin' seems normal. Until you gets to the bridge."

"Bridge?"

"You hears the sound o' runnin' water and suddenly, there's a river, see? A river that shouldn't be there, with a bridge over it. That's 'ow it all starts. With the bridge. And Barry."

"Who?"

"Old Barry the Troll. He's the bridge keeper. All smelly an' stinkin' an' covered in slime."

"Riiiiight," said Clover. "Yes, I suppose that'd be a pretty big clue."

"Can't miss 'im; he's got a tree growin' out of 'is head. That's his idea of a hairdo." Mrs. Eckles gave a disapproving sniff. "Never prunes it, lets it go wild. Gives you a turn when he leaps out roarin'. He can't help it, they all do that. It's a Troll thing."

"Uncontrollable, then," said Clover, quite wittily, she thought. But Mrs. Eckles didn't laugh. "Sorry, go on, I'm listening."

"Give 'im a minute, then he'll calm down and get down to business."

"What business?"

"He asks you three questions. Or *Questions Three*, as he likes to put it. Get 'em right and you can cross the bridge."

"What if you get them wrong?"

"You can't, it's common knowledge. He asks you 'is name, 'is favorite color, and what he 'ad for breakfast. The answers are Barry, brown, and fish. Anyone can get by. He's stupid as a brick."

"So why bother having him?"

"Probably just for show. He's bloomin' ugly."

Clover thought about this for a bit. Mrs. Eckles sometimes came out with the most surprising bits of information.

"This Path," said Clover. "It comes and goes, does it?"

"Yep. Might not see it for years, or it might turn up three nights runnin'. Never in the same place twice. You're hurryin' along, thinkin' you're nearly 'ome, then all of a sudden, Old Barry's in yer face. You can do without it, especially when yer dyin' for a bathroom."

"So what do you do? Answer the questions?"

"Absolutely not," said Mrs. Eckles, firmly. *"Do not engage.* You 'ave a choice, see. You gotta *choose* to take the Path. It can't make you. If you speak, you'll get *involved.* Just button yer lip, turn around, and backtrack. Don't look past Barry, whatever you do, or you'll want to know what lies over the bridge. Curiosity killed the cat." Neville gave another little shiver in his sleep.

"What *does* lie over the bridge?" asked Clover.

"You see?" Mrs. Eckles chuckled and leaned over to poke the fire. "You're curious. But don't ask me. Like I say, I've never walked the Perilous Path. Well, only as far as Barry, for research purposes. But no farther."

"I don't blame you. Why put yourself in peril?"

"It's not so much that. It's more—well, it's a dodgy road to take, if you're a Witch. It can *change you.* Bring out the worst side. Go too far along, and there's a good chance you'll end up as one of the perils yerself. My grandmother went some way along it once. When my sister and me was kids, before she retired."

"Did she?" Clover wasn't surprised. She had only met Mrs. Eckles's incredibly ancient, exceedingly scary grandmother once, quite briefly, but that was more than enough. Even on short acquaintance, you could tell she was the type to experimentally walk a Perilous Path. "Did she say what it was like?"

"Nope. Never talked about it. But I remember she was in a funny mood when she returned. Shut 'erself away for days, writin' stuff down in 'er private spell book. Threw trays at the footmen, shouted a lot. I 'ad a feelin' she didn't want to come back. It ain't a good road, Clover. So don't take it."

"I wasn't planning to. I'm never out in the woods after sundown."

"I know. Anyway, enough o' that. I've told you, and now you know. Saturday night—time you got your wages."

Mrs. Eckles twiddled her fingers. Instantly, the lamps brightened. The fire crackled as cheerful flames caught a log. Neville rolled over to have his tummy tickled. Outside, the wind cut off mid-blow, and suddenly, everything was back to normal. Mrs. Eckles heaved herself from her chair, took an old, cracked teapot from the mantelpiece, and counted out six pennies into Clover's palm.

"There. Four for yer ma, two for you, right?"

"Thanks," said Clover.

"You're off to see 'em all tomorrow, right?"

"First thing in the morning."

"Take 'em a few eggs. I'll give you a bottle o' my special tonic for yer ma, the proper stuff, not the sugar water. And tell you what, I'm feelin' generous. You can have that leftover apple pie."

"Well, that's very good of you," said Clover, "seeing as how I made it."

"Don't be snarky. Well, I'm off to bed, I'll leave you to damp the fire an' lock up. I'll see you tomorrow night. Don't be late comin' back. Before sunset, you hear?"

"Before sunset," promised Clover. At that point, she meant it.

CHAPTER TWO

Clover's Day Off

It was early the next morning and once again Clover was hurrying through the woods, her basket full of presents for the family. Tonic and four precious pennies for Ma, the half pie, a small jar of something green that smelled vile but would kill head lice, six eggs, honey, and a big bag of sweets for the kids. She also had a new hat for Little Herby. It was a red woolly one with flaps to keep his ears warm in the winter. She had knitted it herself, helped by Mrs. Eckles. She hoped he'd like it but had a feeling he'd be more thrilled about the sweets.

Clover had bought the sweets out of her savings. She couldn't wait to see their faces. She had shown them to Mrs. Eckles, who had twiddled her fingers over the bag and said, briskly, "There. That'll make 'em last longer."

"Why? Have you put a never-emptying spell on the bag or something?"

"'Course not. Give kids never-endin' sweets, think I'm mad?"

Clover had peered in the bag and found that each sweet was now wrapped in a twist of brightly colored shiny paper. It would certainly make them last longer, what with having to peel the fiddly wrappers off. This was sensible magic, the kind that Clover approved of.

"I've made 'em taste better, too," said Mrs. Eckles. "Not just strawberry. *Interestin'* flavors. Special. They'll like 'em. "

Clover had been sorely tempted to try one but managed to resist. If they were as good as all that, she had the feeling that she'd scoff the lot and feel guilty for the rest of her life.

"Hey, Clover! Cloooo-verrrrr!"

She turned around at the call. Wilf came hurrying up the track with a box of groceries, waving and yelling. His boot caught on a tree root, knocking him off balance. The box slid from his grasp and fell to the ground with the sound of breaking eggs. A round loaf rolled off into a nearby ditch, picking up dirt and small twigs as it went. Wilf was naturally clumsy, which is why his knees were always scabby and his head covered in lumps.

"Hello," said Clover. "Good trip?"

"Very funny," Wilf said with a groan, rubbing his head and making his red hair stand up. He peered down at the ruined loaf. "Oh, rats! Look at that. Old Trowzer'll take it out of my wages."

"Who's it for?"

"Mrs. Pluck. You know what she's like."

"I do," said Clover. Mrs. Pluck was one of the village gossips. She would take great pleasure in getting Wilf into trouble. They both stared down at the loaf.

"Mrs. Pluck is out of luck," said Clover.

"Her loaf has landed in the muck," contributed Wilf, and they both sniggered.

"Where are you off to? Home?" asked Wilf.

"Yep."

"I'll come with you as far as the turn-off. I'm going that way."

But it wasn't that simple. When Wilf attempted to pick up the box, the bottom fell out, depositing the groceries on the ground. Clover had to fix it with the length of string she always carried in her apron pocket. Then she neatly repacked it with the bags of tea and sugar, the jars of pickles and honey, and lots of slippery little packages wrapped in oiled paper. They left the cracked eggs and the loaf behind.

"What's in your basket?" asked Wilf as they set off. "Anything to eat?"

"No," said Clover quickly. Wilf was always hungry. He ate anything, except for tomatoes, which he claimed reminded him of eyeballs.

"You're lying, aren't you?"

"Yes, well, all right, I've got some sweets for the kids."

"Let's have one."

"Certainly not. They're special. Mrs. Eckles did something to them."

"Even better. Come on, let's have one."

"No."

"Ah, come on. Just one. Give me one and I'll shut up. Look, I'm begging. Come on. Just one. Come on—come on—come on—come on—come on—"

"All right," said Clover, relenting. "You can have one, but not yet."

And Wilf had to make do with that.

"How's Mrs. Eckles?" he asked, to take his mind off things.

"All right. How's your grampy?"

"Same as ever. Grumpy."

"You haven't been around in a while."

"Why, did you miss me?"

"Like a hole in the head," said Clover, although she had, a bit.

"Lot of deliveries this week. Old Trowzer's kept me busy. I've got two more after this, miles apart. Yesterday, I went to three separate places and nobody was even *home*, so no tips. Not even a cup of tea. *Ow!*"

Wilf walked into a low branch, banging his eye. Clover winced.

"Didn't you get paid?" she asked.

"Already paid for. Old Trowzer said to leave 'em in the shed. So, tell me. Anything happened lately? Any— you know. *Magical* goings-on?"

"No," said Clover. "Not really."

"I wouldn't like to miss out on anything."

"You haven't. It's been really quiet. Mrs. Eckles says it's too warm for Witchcraft. She does the protection spells on Friday nights and spends the rest of her time puttering around the garden."

This was true. Although Clover didn't bother mentioning that the watering can could usually be seen clanking along at Mrs. Eckles's heels, pausing occasionally to helpfully sprinkle, like a small, faithful dog. Wilf already knew that. He knew about the talking gate too. There are things you learn to take for granted when you spend time around Witches.

"She hasn't mentioned taking the cottage up again, then? For a spin?"

"No."

"No more cakes on the doorstep? No attempted break-ins?" Wilf lowered his voice. "By You Know Who?"

"If you mean Mesmeranza, no. She's gone all quiet."

"Sssh," said Wilf, glancing nervously around. "You shouldn't say her name. The trees have ears."

"No they don't, don't be so silly."

"Well, it's bad luck."

"No such thing," said Clover. "Mrs. Eckles says people make their own luck. Anyway, she never mentions her now. Well, she did yesterday, when Granny Dismal visited, but that's because she was desperate for something to say."

"Granny Dismal visited?"

"Yes. She came to warn us about a Perilous Path in the woods."

"She would," said Wilf. "Loves to spread bad news, that one. Er—*what* Perilous Path?"

"It's a long story," said Clover. For some reason she didn't want to talk about the Path on a sunny morning. "Just don't stay out after sunset for a while."

"Some hopes of that," said Wilf. "I reckon I won't be home 'til midnight tonight."

"Well, if you come across a bridge over a river with a strange Troll asking questions, just ignore him and walk away."

"A *Troll?* Are you *serious?*"

"You heard. Do not engage. That's what Mrs. Eckles said. Anyway, there's been no word from Mesmeranza. I think they've both moved on to other things. You can't bear grudges forever."

"Good," said Wilf. "That's . . . good." He sounded almost disappointed.

"Yes," said Clover firmly. "It is."

There had been an adventure a while back. It had happened just after Clover began cleaning for Mrs. Eckles. A lot of unsettling things had occurred—in particular, an almighty family feud involving, among other things, cake, a jealous sister who also happened to be a Witch, a surprise grandmother, hypnotism, an unhelpful Imp, a bottle of magical potion, and the incredible discovery that the cottage *could actually fly*! Not to speak of an uncomfortable period of imprisonment in a castle dungeon, a flying horse called Booboo, and an alarming number of lightning bolts. There were a lot of *bad* bits to the adventure, and by the end, Clover had had quite enough. Wilf had enjoyed it, though. Except for the *really* bad bits. At any rate, he never stopped talking about it.*

"I wish she would," said Wilf. "Take the cottage up again, I mean."

"Why? You hated it. You wouldn't even look down."

"I know. But at least it was something different. Made a change from delivering groceries."

"Well, it's not going to happen," said Clover firmly. "I've got everything nice and tidy now. You know what always happens to the furniture."

"You," said Wilf with a sigh. "You're so . . . *sensible*."

"And what's wrong with that?" asked Clover, rather irritably. He made it sound as though it were a *bad* thing.

---

*If you want to know more, read *Clover Twig and the Magical Cottage*.

27

"Here she is!" shouted Clover's ma. She was standing in the doorway with Little Herby in her arms. As always, he wore his cut-down flour sack, the one with the big red pocket. He was sucking on his comfort rag—a horrible old shawl with tattered red fringing. Clover's three small sisters clustered around Ma's skirts—Fern, Bracken, and Sorrel.

"Covey!" squealed Herby. He wriggled out of Ma's arms and came running unsteadily down the path, face beaming.

"My, Herby! Look at you walking!" marveled Clover, scooping him up and plonking a kiss on his dirty face. Herby joyfully attempted to stuff his rag down her throat, and she hastily put him down.

She hurried up the path to give Ma a hug, followed by each one of her sisters.

"Did you bring us anything?" asked Sorrel, squirming out of her arms.

"I did. " Clover rummaged in her basket and produced the bag of sweets. "Here. Special sweeties." Eight eager little hands reached out. "All right, all right, don't snatch. Fern, you take it. Share them out equally, mind."

"Seeties!" shouted Little Herby, bouncing around. "Want seeties!" Sweets were a rare treat in the Twig household.

"I know you do. Look, I've made you a hat too, to match your pocket." Clover popped it on his head and tied it under his chin. "There. Don't you look smart?"

"Want seeties," said Herby ungratefully.

"And you shall have some. Be a good boy and wait while Fern divides them up." Clover turned to Ma and put her arm around her waist. "Come on, let's go in and put the kettle on."

"There's no tea," said Ma. "I sent Pa out to borrow a twist."

"He'll be in the Axes, then," said Clover.

"Reckon so." Ma gave a sigh. "He knows you're coming home, though, so he won't be long."

Inside, the place was a shambles. The beds were unmade and the kitchen table was piled high with items of ragged clothing and unwashed crockery. The walls were covered with chalk scribbles and wobbly drawings of stick people.

"I know it's a mess," Ma said guiltily. "They keep scribblin' on the walls with chalk. The peddler came by and gave 'em a free box. I wish he hadn't. I need eyes in the back of me head, now that Herby's walking properly. He keeps running off after butterflies. It'd help if your pa would fix that gate. It's off the hinges again. He says I make too much fuss. *You won't say that when a wolf gets him, I say.*"

"A wolf won't get him," soothed Clover. Automatically, she began picking up the bedclothes and folding them into a neat pile.

"So how's it going, then?" asked Ma. "Things all right, are they?"

Ma spoke hesitantly. She still wasn't too comfortable with the fact that her daughter worked for a Witch. She didn't ask questions about the witchy side of things at all, and Clover was glad about that. If she knew the truth, she'd have had a fit.

"Yep. She sent some eggs and honey. And a bottle of tonic for you. And there's half a pie and some stuff to put on the kids' heads."

"Well, that's good of her. I've noticed 'em itching."

"And here's the money." Clover reached into her basket, took out a little cloth purse, and placed it in Ma's outstretched palm.

"Thanks, love," said Ma, dropping it into her pocket, suddenly a lot more cheerful. "There's quite a bit of news. You know Tilly Adams, what works at the Axes? She's run off with the peddler man."

"The one who gives out free chalk?"

"The very one. Her dad's that mad."

"I'm not surprised, Tilly being his only daughter," said Clover, fetching the broom.

"It's not that. He bought a fryin' pan from him and the handle came off. And you know Tobe Thomas? He's been laid off work. Chronic ear wax. And remember Gammer Warty's Daisy, the cow with the crumpled horn? It got out of the field and it took her three days to catch it. . ."

Clover let her run on. She was still talking and Clover was still sweeping when a shadow fell across the doorway and Pa's voice said, "Well, well. If it's not my favorite eldest daughter!"

"Hello, Pa," said Clover, and gave him a kiss on his stubbly chin. She caught a strong whiff of ale. Yes, he had been to the Axes.

"Did you get the tea?" asked Ma.

"I did," said Pa, triumphantly producing a small package from his pocket. "Put the kettle on, Clover, and tell yer old dad what you been up to. How's old mother Eckles?"

"Fine. She sent half a pie and some eggs."

"Did she now? Well, that's right kind of her. I wouldn't say no to a slice o' pie."

"I'll call the kids in," said Ma. "They'd like a bit too, I expect. Fern! Bracken! Sorrel! Herby! Come on in, there's pie!"

There came the sound of running feet, and the girls appeared in the doorway. All three had over-excited, sticky faces with bulging cheeks.

"Where's Herby?" inquired Ma.

The girls looked at each other and shrugged.

"We was playin' hide and seek," said Sorrel. "He went to hide."

"Oh my!" Ma said with a sigh. "If you've let him run off again . . ." She hurried to the door and looked out. "Herby? Where are you?"

Silence.

"No sign of 'im," said Ma. "See what I mean, Clover?"

"I'll find him," said Clover. "He'll be behind the gooseberry bushes."

But Herby wasn't behind the gooseberries. She searched under every bush, behind the water barrel, and even poked her nose in the privy. She looked behind the garden gate, which was propped uselessly to one side. Trees pressed thickly against the fence, which had collapsed in places.

"Herby?" shouted Clover into the trees. "Come on in now, game's over."

But there was no reply.

"Any sign?" said Ma, coming up from behind.

"No. I suppose we'll have to look in the woods. Don't worry, he can't have gone far."

"He might have gone to Mrs. Pickles's place," said Ma. "She lets him hold the baby chicks." She untied her apron, dropped it on the ground, and went hurrying off.

"More likely gone to the rope swing down by the brook," said Pa, coming down the path with a slice of pie in his hand. "He's not allowed, but try tellin' him that."

"We'll help look," said Fern, running up with Sorrel and Bracken. All three of them looked excited, as if this were a game.

"No," said Clover, firmly. "You stay here in case he comes back. Pa'll go to the rope swing, and I'll try over by the rabbit warren."

But Herby wasn't at Mrs. Pickles's place or at the rope swing or at the rabbit warren. The three of them met up back at the garden gate, feeling anxious but trying not to show it. "I know!" shouted Ma. "He'll be down at Farmer Crocker's field. He likes to climb on the gate and stare at the billy goat. That's where he is!"

They set off for Farmer Crocker's field. But there was no little figure hanging over the five-bar gate. If the goat had recently been stared at by Herby, it certainly wasn't letting on.

They searched in ever-increasing circles, going deeper

and deeper into the woods, calling and calling. Ma sent Fern off to make inquiries at the village—but no one had seen him there.

Noon came and went, and still there was no sign. Pa went to the Crossed Axes and enlisted the help of his drinking pals. For once, he didn't stop for a pint himself. By mid-afternoon, the word had spread, and more and more locals joined in the search. Nobody stopped to eat or rest. The woods rang with far-off cries.

"Herby . . . Herby . . ."

By sundown, the terrible truth finally sank in. Little Herby was missing.

The family met in the cottage as the sky turned red. Pa looked pale and grim. Ma was a trembling wreck. The girls looked scared and not so excited now. In fact, they were suspiciously quiet.

"What's up with you three?" demanded Clover. "Is there something you're not telling us?"

The girls looked at each other and said nothing.

"Come on," said Clover. "Out with it."

"He tooked all the *sweeties*," said Sorrel, and burst into tears. Fern and Bracken joined in, and try as she would, Clover couldn't get another word out of them.

"You'd best be getting back, Clover," said Pa. "Sun's going down."

"Not until we've found him," said Clover.

"You can't do any more. A group of us are meeting at the Axes and going out with torches."

"Then I'm coming too."

"No," said Pa, firmly. "The best thing you can do is go and tell Mrs. Eckles. She might be able to help. Study the tea leaves, consult the stars, I dunno."

"Pa's right," sniffed Ma, through her tears. "Calls herself a Witch, don't she? She's got powers, right? She could look in a Crystal Ball or something, couldn't she?"

"I don't know," said Clover. "Maybe."

Mrs. Eckles didn't have a Crystal Ball, of course; she didn't approve of them. And the business with the tea leaves and stars was a load of rubbish, she admitted that herself. But she did have powers. Telling her made sense.

"I'll be back first thing tomorrow, at sunup," promised Clover. She placed a comforting arm around Ma's shaking shoulders. "Don't worry, he'll turn up."

She tried to sound cheerful and positive, but the words sounded hollow.

"Take a lantern," said Pa. "We don't want you getting lost an' all."

"All right. But I'll be there by dusk if I hurry."

"Just in case," said Pa. He took a lantern off a hook and handed it to her.

She hugged them, one by one, picked up her basket, and set off once again into the woods, which were bathed in an orange glow.

And the sun dropped below the horizon.

CHAPTER THREE

Send for the Huntsman!

And now we must leave Clover and travel far away from the forest to a very different place.

There is no orange glow to the sky above Castle Coldiron. The castle stands on the topmost peak in an area of towering, jagged mountains and deep, dark canyons. Some of the mountains are tipped with snow.

Here, the sky is always gray. The sun is buried behind banked clouds. When night comes, the gray just darkens to black.

"Still no sign?" snapped Mesmeranza.

Ah. Here she is at last. Mrs. Eckles's infamous sister. She is currently sitting in a high-backed chair in her turret room. Set beside her, on a small, polished table, is a Crystal Ball. It is one of the old-fashioned ones, the size and shape of a small goldfish bowl. Right now it contains nothing but gray mist.

Mesmeranza has a pale, heavily powdered face and her black hair is swept back and up and secured with a comb. Her lips are painted the same violent shade of red as her long, sharp nails. Her gown is green satin. It matches her shoes. Her eyes are green too. The same emerald as Mrs. Eckles's eyes—but harder.

It is there that the resemblance ends. Mrs. Eckles has allowed herself to grow old. Mesmeranza hasn't. She maintains her deceptively youthful looks with the help of a Mirror Of Eternal Youth, which deals magically with aging issues. These days, the sessions are getting much longer.

"No," sighed the small, gray, frazzled-looking woman who was standing next to the window, staring out. "No sign."

This is Miss Fly speaking, and she is a cat lover. You can tell by the state of her shapeless cardigan, which is thickly plastered with hair. She houses the cats in her apartment, where they sleep, eat, yowl, fight, have kittens, and commandeer her bed. She is allowed to keep them in exchange for what are described as "light secretarial duties." Miss Fly doesn't like the job, but it's not easy to find accommodation when you have over forty fluffy friends.

"This is ridiculous," said Mesmeranza. "He should have been back hours ago. Send for him again."

"I've already sent for him three times. He hasn't arrived, I would have seen him from the window."

"He's flying in on Booboo. He'll be coming from the stables around the back. *Do it.*"

Miss Fly shrugged and trudged to the door. She opened it and cleared her throat.

"Ahem. Send for the huntsman!" squeaked Miss Fly.

Her thin quaver echoed down a long flight of stairs and along distant corridors. A second voice took up the cry, then another, then another. The calls got fainter and fainter until they faded away to silence.

"You see?" said Miss Fly.

"Don't sound so *pleased*, Fly," snapped Mesmeranza. "It's in your own interests that the fool arrives, because

40

you certainly won't be leaving until he does. He and I have business to conduct. I may need your assistance."

"What business?" inquired Miss Fly. She glanced at her watch. The cats would be wanting their supper.

"He has something for me. Something I require for my latest Plan."

"Plan?" Miss Fly's voice held an element of dread. "You have a new Plan?"

"I most certainly do. I've been working on it for some time now."

"It wouldn't have anything to do with stealing flying cottages, by any chance?"

"No. How many times must I tell you, Fly? I've lost interest in the wretched cottage. And I didn't steal it. I prefer the word *reclaim*."

"Whatever you call it, your sister got it back," Miss Fly reminded her.

"Yes, and she's welcome to it. It's a dump."

"So what is it, then? This new Plan?"

"Why should I tell you? You'll only pour cold water on it, as usual. You don't have to know all the details of every Plan I come up with. I'm quite capable of creative planning without your involvement."

"You usually involve me," pointed out Miss Fly. "You make me take notes and do all the running around."

"Yes, and all the while I have to listen to your constant *carping*. Right now I don't need your doomy forebodings. The Plan is all worked out and ready to go."

"But you're not going to tell me what it is."

"All right," sighed Mesmeranza. "If you *must* know, there is something I need to get my hands on. Something that belonged to Grandmother that's rightfully mine."

"Really?" Miss Fly sounded surprised. "I thought you said you inherited everything. The castle, the servants, all those dangerous old magical items up in the loft. . ."

"I did, and quite right too. But there's one thing missing. The Bad Spell Book."

"Bad Spell Book?" said Miss Fly. "What Bad Spell Book? You've never mentioned it before."

"Well, I don't tell you everything, do I? I remember it from when Demelza and I were children. Grandmother wrote all her nastiest, most powerful spells down in a book. We weren't allowed near it. She kept it in her private laboratory; we could hear it creeping about, rustling its pages at night. But it's not there now. In fact, it's nowhere in the castle. Believe me, I've looked."

"Perhaps she destroyed it," said Miss Fly. "Or lost it. Maybe she took it with her to the Twilight Home."

"*Wrong!*" Mesmeranza gave a triumphant smirk. "I

know exactly where it is. It's in the cottage. Hidden under a loose flagstone by the hearth."

"How did you find that out?"

"Very easily. I paid Grandmother a little visit. Took her a bunch of grapes and a small cactus."

"I thought you parted on bad terms. After the business with the cottage."

"We did. I can't say she was pleased to see me. Told me what I could do with my thoughtful gifts and ordered me to leave and never darken her doorstep again, which I was only too glad to do. They keep that place horribly overheated. But not before she spilled the beans and told me where the book is."

"What—she just came right out with it?"

"Oh, yes. You see, I had the foresight to doctor the grapes with Instant Truth Serum. I used her own recipe, actually. Tasteless, odorless, completely undetectable. She showed us how to make it once, back when we were children and she was training us up. I think she's forgotten. I soaked the cactus in it too, just to be on the safe side."

"Well, I must say I'm surprised," said Miss Fly. "I thought she was the suspicious type. That's what you told me. You said it was impossible to put one over on her."

"Yes, well, I picked my moment. I waited until the tea trolley appeared and she started bellowing for tea and cookies along with the rest of the residents. I simply popped a grape in her mouth and wafted the cactus under her nose, and she went all glassy-eyed and told me everything. I found her wand too, hidden in her knitting bag. They don't allow dangerous weapons in the Twilight Home, so I took it. Then I left, before the trolley arrived."

"All right," said Miss Fly, "all right, so you've found out this horrid book is in the cottage. What will you do? Visit your sister and ask her nicely?"

"Are you mad?" said Mesmeranza, sneering. "Demelza and I don't *do* nice."

"Well, perhaps you should. It's silly. Keeping up a vendetta at your age."

"I *beg* your pardon? Did you just *mention my age?*"

"Sorry," said Miss Fly hastily, aware that she had stepped into dangerous waters.

"You go too far!"

"Sorry. But I'm just saying. It might save time. Your sister's more into—you know—healing herbs and woodland lore. What would she want with a book of bad spells? That's more your sort of thing."

"Exactly! With that book, there's nothing I can't do.

Make it rain snakes for seven years. Turn the footmen into purple lizards. Cause a plague of giant flying cockroaches. An invasion of hostile hedgehogs. A pimple epidemic. Whatever takes my fancy."

"Well, I don't see your sister being interested. She might be happy to give it to you."

"What an innocent you are, Fly. Do you really think Demelza would hand it over, just like that? Beautifully gift-wrapped, perhaps? There is a reason the book is in the cottage. Grandmother wanted to keep it safe from *me*. Some dreary old nonsense about the balance of good and evil."

"Oh, right. So that's that, then," said Miss Fly.

"No, Fly. That is *not* that. Obviously I intend to seize it back."

"But the cottage is wired up with protection spells. You can't cross the threshold, can you? You can't trick your way in again. They're wise to you now, after what happened back in the spring."

"I'm aware of that, Fly. That's why I have a new Plan. What's that you're eating?"

"It's an allergy pill," explained Miss Fly, holding up a small pot. "A new sort from the chemist. I have to take three a day."

"And are they working?"

"Well, yes. My nose isn't as stuffed up as usual."

"If you got rid of the wretched beasts you wouldn't have to take them."

"Maybe," said Miss Fly, adding nobly, "but think of the sacrifice. Where would I be without Oliver and Tabitha and Tiddles and Morris and . . . ?"

"Enough of your cats! It's the Bad Spell Book that concerns me now. Once I have that, I shall take great pleasure in getting revenge on both Demelza *and* little Miss Twig. Two for the price of one. A bargain."

"So that's really what all this is about? Getting revenge? You don't think it's time to let it drop?"

"I said I'd get revenge. Those were my last words to them. *I'll be back!* I said."

"That could mean anything," pointed out Miss Fly. "You could have gone back for a cup of tea, or to collect for charity, or—"

"I'm *getting revenge!*" shouted Mesmeranza, banging the chair arm with her fist. "I'm getting it, and that's that. Clover Twig made me look like a fool. Showing me up in front of Grandmother, it's unforgivable. She's every bit as much to blame as Demelza, and she will *pay.* As soon as I get that book."

"And how do you intend to do that?" inquired Miss Fly. "What's the huntsman got to do with it?"

"Ah. Now, here's the thing. I have ordered him to kidnap Clover Twig's little brother. Once he's in my clutches, I shall send her a letter advising her that if she wants to see him again, she will secretly remove the book from its hiding place, bring it out of the cottage, and deliver it into my hands. I shall then seize her, bring her back here to Coldiron, and throw her in the dungeon where she belongs. I won't tell her that last bit, of course. That'll come as a complete surprise."

"But—that's *wicked!*" said Miss Fly, gasping. "Using innocent little children to further your own ends!"

"Fly," said Mesmeranza, exasperated, "how many times must I tell you? Young Miss Twig may be a child, but a very irritating one who needs to be taught a lesson. And that lesson is"—she leaned forward, eyes flashing—"*never cross me.*"

"But using the little brother as bait. It isn't right!"

"He's the means to an end. Stop being so sentimental . . . ah! At last."

There came the sound of approaching footsteps echoing down a corridor, accompanied by heavy panting. The footsteps halted at the door. There came a hesitant knock.

"Enter," called Mesmeranza.

The door opened and in squelched the huntsman, hot and bothered and dripping with sweat.

The huntsman's name was Hybrow Hunter. Hunter because that was the family name, and Hybrow because his mother had hopeful plans for him. Sadly, Hybrow had shown no talent for art, music, poetry, law, medicine, or architecture and ended up as a huntsman with a silly name, as his brothers, Blud and Gory, never failed to remind him.

Right now, however, Hybrow's name was the last thing on his mind. His green hat kept slithering to one side, such was the flow of nervous perspiration from his pores, and his tights clung to his thighs in a very unpleasant manner.

There were two reasons for this. First, Hybrow had just endured a very long, nerve-wracking flight on a flying horse, who sped like the devil, dive-bombing treetops on purpose in order to scrape Hybrow's knees; reared at bats; snapped at owls; nearly threw him on more than one occasion; then whacked him around the head with a wing when he finally dismounted. The horse's name was Booboo, although Hybrow had called it some other names in the course of the flight.

Second, his employer had entrusted him with an unpleasant but exceedingly generously paid task. A whole

bag of gold, in fact! Just to do one simple task. A task *that he had failed to perform.* Hybrow's head was awash with the lies he intended to tell so he wouldn't get into trouble and still get the gold. He had been working on them the whole journey back. He hoped he'd get the story straight. He couldn't bear to think about what might happen if he messed up.

"Approach," commanded Mesmeranza.

Hybrow swept off his slippery hat, bowed, and damply approached. Rivulets of sweat dripped from his beard. His huntsman's horn clanked dully against his knee. The dagger in his belt was digging into his side.

"Sorry I'm late, milady," he said, panting and fingering his too-tight tunic neck. "Transport problems."

"Is that so? I've been waiting for *hours*."

"Booboo was acting up. Ran into a load of bats. Had to make a detour. Not exactly what you'd call a *smooth* ride."

"You look hot, Master Hunter," said Miss Fly. "Your beard is dripping. Shall I ring for some iced tea?"

"Why, thank you, that'd be very—"

"What are you *thinking*, Fly?" cut in Mesmeranza, curtly. "This isn't a café. The man is here to report to me, not sip luxuriously on cold drinks. Come along, man, don't keep me waiting. Did you get the bait? Yes or no?"

"What, the kid?" said Hybrow, innocently. He took a handkerchief from his jerkin and mopped his brow, partly because it needed mopping but mainly so he didn't have to meet her fierce gaze. "Oh yes, I got him."

This wasn't exactly a lie. He *had* got him, to begin with. To begin with, it had all gone according to plan. Hybrow had leaped from the bushes, scooped up the kid, ran to where Booboo was waiting, and almost had him over the saddle. It had so nearly been the perfect kidnapping.

And then the little tyke bit him! Really hard, on the finger! While Hybrow was dancing around screaming, the slippery little devil had wriggled off under the bushes, never to be seen again.

"*Hah!*" Gleefully, Mesmeranza punched the arm of her chair. "Where? Where is it?"

"Back home in the Lodge, " said Hybrow.

Now, this was a *proper* lie. Little Herby wasn't back in the Lodge. Little Herby was hiding somewhere in the woods. Hybrow had blundered around looking for him for hours, only giving in when too many other people began showing up. It wouldn't do to be seen.

They would notice a stranger, particularly one accompanied by an evil-looking horse with a conspicuous set of large, feathery wings. So Hybrow had abandoned the search and flown home Herby-less, cursing his luck.

"Why the Lodge?" demanded Mesmeranza. "Why didn't you bring it here, as instructed?"

"Him," Miss Fly corrected her. "Not *it*."

"Be quiet, Fly. Nobody's asking you."

"Mum's giving him a bath," lied Hybrow. "She thinks he's got nits." This was inspired. Hybrow was pleased with this.

"*Nits?*" Mesmeranza gave a little shriek of dismay. Both she and Miss Fly stared in horror. Automatically, their hands flew to their heads.

"Yes. I didn't think you'd want to see him yet, milady. Until they're gone."

"I certainly don't," agreed Mesmeranza, vigorously scratching her scalp. "You'd better keep it with you for the time being."

Hybrow began to relax. So far, all was going according to plan. Perhaps he would get away with it. Get away with it, take the money, and run. Be several counties away before she discovered the truth. Whole *countries* away would be better.

"By the way," Mesmeranza went on, "I take it you've got proof?"

"Proof, milady?"

"Yes, proof! Proof that you've got little whatshisname."

"Herby," said Miss Fly. "His name's Little Herby, short for Herbediah."

"Yes, yes, whatever. *Do* stop interrupting, Fly, I'm trying to do business here." Mesmeranza glared at Hybrow. "No proof, no pay. For all I know, you could be pulling the wool over my eyes. You could have taken *pity* and let it go, like the fool who was ordered to deal with that ninny Snow White."

"*He* brought back proof," Miss Fly told them. "A boar's heart, as I recall."

"Yes, but it was *fake* proof, wasn't it? He brought back *fake* proof in the vain hope he could fool the Queen."

"Imagine!" Hybrow shook his head, trying to appear scandalized. "Lettin' us huntsmen down like that, the treacherous toe rag."

"Quite. So give me proof you've got the bait. I want *proper* proof. Don't try palming off a handful of boar innards on me."

Hybrow fished in his pouch with a clammy hand.

Everything hinged on this. He withdrew a filthy rag with a tattered red fringe. Here and there were pale patches where it had been sucked slightly cleaner.

"Here," he said, holding it out.

"Ugh! What is it?" squealed Mesmeranza, shrinking away.

"It's his bit of rag. Drags it everywhere."

"It looks like it." Mesmeranza gave a shudder. "Take it, Fly."

"Me?"

"Yes, you. You don't think *I'm* going to handle the disgusting thing, do you?"

Miss Fly gingerly took the rag, holding it by one edge between thumb and forefinger.

"So there's your proof," said Hybrow. "You can't get better proof than that."

"Hmm. Yes, well, all right, I suppose you can go. Go back and wait for further instructions."

Hybrow lingered. He shuffled from foot to foot, fiddling with his hat.

"I think he wants payment," said Miss Fly. "He did the job. It's only fair."

"Oh very well, pay him off. The gold's in the chest. And put that awful thing where I can't see it."

Miss Fly scuttled to a chest in the corner, raised the

lid, dropped in the offending rag, rummaged around, and took out a clinking bag. She handed it to Mesmeranza, who handed it to Hybrow, who tried not to snatch it too eagerly.

"Thanks, milady," he said. "Best get home, see how mum's coping with the lil' guy." And he hurried from the room.

"Right," said Mesmeranza, as the sound of his footsteps died away. "To work. Got your pencil, Fly? I want you to take a letter."

CHAPTER FOUR

What Happened to Little Herby?

Darkness comes quickly in the woods—and right now, the woods were very dark indeed. Dark, deep, and silent.

A bush shook. There came the sound of heavy breathing—and Little Herby crawled out!

He was horrendously filthy. His sack was stained

beyond belief, and his new red hat was full of leaves and twigs. Multicolored goo encrusted his face from hairline to chin. The gunk beneath his fingernails alone could have kept scientists busy for years. As for his small, bare feet—well! It looked like he had mud socks on.

Herby climbed unsteadily to his feet and stood rubbing his eyes and yawning. He had needed the nap, short as it was, because the day had held a lot of strange experiences for such a little boy.

The morning had started wonderfully well, because Clover had arrived with sweeties. Herby loved Clover and missed her when she was away. Combined with sweeties, the sight of her had been almost too much pleasure to bear.

The pleasure had faded when the sweeties were counted out. Fern, Sorrel, and Bracken had taken *loads* more than him, he knew. They had filled their pockets, then meanly given him just one for each hand. When he objected, they forced open his fingers and took the two back again. Then they pushed him over, ran off, and hid the bag behind the water barrel. They thought he was howling into his comfort rag, which he was, but Herby was no fool. He saw where they put it.

When the girls came back, they were in a much

better mood. Their cheeks were bulging, and their eyes were wide and sparkling. To keep him from crying, Fern had unwrapped a single sweet—it had a red wrapper—and popped it into his open mouth.

Herby had never tasted anything so wonderful! It tasted of strawberries and raspberries and sun-dried tomatoes combined with rubies. He had never tasted any of these things and certainly couldn't put a name to them—but my, that red sweet tasted amazing!

To keep up his improved mood, Fern suggested hide-and-seek, which was his favorite game, now that he'd gotten the hang of it and stopped helpfully calling out his position whenever the seeker approached. Silence was the rule.

Still sucking his wonderful red sweet, Herby trotted off to hide in the gooseberry bushes. Then, while the girls' backs were turned, he crawled over to the water barrel and snatched the hidden bag. Breathing heavily with excitement, he stuffed it into the red pocket that Ma had sewn onto the front of his sack. Herby kept things in the pocket, along with a year's worth of crumbs and old food droppings. He kept his comfort rag there when he wasn't using it, along with a pet worm called Wiggly and a stick of red chalk. All his best stuff.

Then he set off into the woods.

Things began looking up at this point. Herby had his rag, his chalk, his worm, a new red hat, a big bag of sweets, and freedom, which is all a toddler wants.

But things took a sharp turn down again when a nasty man with a feathered hat jumped out from behind a bush, tucked him under his arm, and attempted to sling him over the saddle of a funny-looking horsey with wings!

Little Herby had three mean sisters and was used to sticking up for himself. He bit the nasty man's finger. The nasty man said a bad word and let go. Herby saw his chance, dropped to all fours, and made for the near-est thicket, where it was dark and tangled and there happened to be a convenient hole. A tiny little secret cave, made by a badger or a fox or something.

Herby knew about hide-and-seek. He didn't shout out. He just crawled in and curled up quietly, holding his breath, until the crashings and cursings ceased, and the nasty man finally went away, taking the horsey with him.

That was good. What wasn't good was the fact that Herby's comfort rag was gone! It had fallen from his pocket when the nasty man dropped him.

Ma was always trying to separate Herby from his rag. She had told him that big boys don't need rags. But

Herby loved his rag. He loved the feel of it and the smell of it and the taste. The crusty bits and the soggy bits and the friendly holes.

Oh well. He would tell Pa about the nasty man, and Pa would find him and make him give the rag back. In the meantime, he would be a big boy and do without it for a little while. At least he had sweeties to compensate.

At this point, Herby left his hidey hole and began walking. He didn't know which way home was, but he wasn't bothered. It was still early. He often wandered off. Someone always eventually came and found him.

Herby liked it in the sun-speckled woods, especially with the sweeties for company. They were so, so lovely. The wrappers were tough to get off, but such beautiful colors. He tried a yellow sweet. It tasted of bananas, gingerbread, and sunshine. That kept him happy for some time. Then he had a green one, which tasted of kiwi fruits and apples and alpine meadows. Herby kept the wrappers, holding each one to his eye to see the world miraculously change color. He carefully smoothed them out and put them into his pocket. He would play a game with them later. He would wrap up small stones and trick Fern and Sorrel and Bracken into thinking they were real, ha-ha!

Chortling to himself at the thought of his little joke,

Herby wandered on. As the day got hotter, his head became a bit warm in his new hat, but he couldn't take it off because he couldn't untie bows. Anyway, it was a present.

What a lovely time he was having! Butterflies fluttered by. A little rabbit popped out its head. Squirrels chattered from the branches. There was a little pool. He broke off a twig and pretended to fish for a bit, but got bored and moved on.

At one point, he stopped and picked some flowers, but they wilted so he threw them away. Another time, he stopped to watch an interesting worm crawl out from under a log, then interestingly crawl back again. After some hesitation, he took Wiggly from his pocket and placed him under the log. Perhaps they would become best friends. Wiggly had lost his novelty value recently. In the last few days, he had gone all dry and stopped doing things.

Farther on, Herby saw some ants and gave them a crumb of rock-hard bread from the depths of his pocket. They didn't seem that interested. In fact, they went out of their way to avoid it. He ate another sweet. This one was purple and tasted like plums and grapes and beetroot mixed with twilight, which may sound weird but was actually absolutely delicious.

He saw a ladybug and blew on her until she flew away home. He ran at some crows and tried to make them fly away too, but they just jeered at him. He whacked at tree trunks with sticks. When his legs got tired, he sat down in sunny glades to have a little breather before toddling on again.

And so the day wore on. The woods were thicker now. There were fewer butterflies and no rabbits. Fewer flowers and more prickly bushes. There was a shortage of sunny glades. There were no birds, either, and no comfortable little scurryings and scuttles of woodland creatures going about their business. It had all gone very quiet. At one point, he thought he could hear distant voices shouting his name—but they were very far away. Suddenly, lovely though they were, Herby didn't want any more sweeties. He wanted bread and milk and a cuddle from Ma.

He seemed to be in an *older* part of the forest. The trees were taller and more gnarly, with exposed roots, like giant, witchy fingers. The ground was marshy. Mud bubbled up between his toes. There was no sign of a main track—just tiny, narrow little paths made by invisible wild things.

Herby was getting tired now. His eyes were feeling heavy. The rare shafts of sunlight that filtered through the trees had an orange glow.

So Herby found a bush and crawled under it. He curled up and dozed off, hugging the bag of sweets, which still felt reassuringly full.

That was two hours ago. Now he was awake. The woods were pitch-black, and he was lost.

"Mama?" he quavered. "Covey?"

Silence.

Herby stared around. As his eyes became accustomed to the dark, he slowly began to make out dim shapes. Tree trunks, mainly, and bushes. Somewhere beyond, he thought he could detect the barest suggestion of light. A faint, silvery glow. Maybe someone was coming with a lantern to rescue him.

"Mama?" Herby tried again. "Here I is, Mama!"

More silence.

With nothing better to do, Herby set off toward the source of the light.

It was closer than he expected. After only a few faltering steps, he was starting to see the way ahead. He could see the pale outline of every tree. Whatever was making the light, it was just around the next bend. As he approached, he became aware of the sound of running water. He rounded a tree . . . and there it was!

A small, wooden bridge spanned a babbling brook. It was set in a glade that was flooded with silver light. That was odd on a moonless night, but Herby was only

little and didn't question it. The water sparkled and chuckled and glittered with stars. The rail of the bridge seemed to be studded with twinkling lights. It looked so pretty, that bridge. Like a bridge in a fairy tale.

"Ooooooh!" breathed Herby, transfixed. He *loved* the look of that bridge. He wanted to run to the middle and hang over the rail and look for little fishies. He wanted to throw twigs into the water and wait for them to float out the other side. He wanted to wave to his own reflection.

Eyes shining, he stepped forward.

There came the sudden cracking of a branch behind him. And a voice in his ear said, *"Pssssssssssst!"*

CHAPTER FIVE

Miss Fly Takes a Letter

"I think that's it," said Mesmeranza. "Read it out once more. I want to make sure I've covered everything."

Miss Fly looked down at her pad, which was covered with scribbles.

"But I've already read it out three tibes."

"I said read it *again*. With more expression this time. You read like a fish. A sort of flat, dull fish. Haddock or something. Give it drama."

"*So, Clover Twig!*" read Miss Fly. "*Tibe for Round Two—*"

"Those new pills of yours," interrupted Mesmeranza. "They've stopped working, haven't they? Your *m*'s are missing."

"I seeb to be losing theb again, yes," admitted poor Miss Fly. It was true. Her nose was beginning to redden and drip, which was always a bad sign.

"Ah me, you and your wretched allergies. What I have to endure. Take another pill."

Miss Fly sniffed and took another pill.

"Say *Mortimer Muffin Moans on Mondays*."

"Bortiber Buffin—"

"Take another one!"

"But it says only three . . ."

"Do it!"

So Miss Fly took another one.

"Try again," ordered Mesmeranza.

"Mortimer Muffin Moans on Mondays," said Miss Fly.

"Right. Continue."

"*So Clover Twig! Time for Round Two. Yes, it's me again, the nasty sister, remember? The one that has 'moved on'—I think* that was how you put it. By the way, trees do have ears, and bad luck happens to everyone. Well, it does when I'm around."

"More drama," insisted Mesmeranza. "Less haddock, more shark. Try gestures."

"I'm *trying*. I'm not good at gestures. Shall I go on?"

"Yes, yes!"

"*To cut to the chase, I have your brother. He is safe and well, but life holds so many twists and turns, does it not? All may yet turn out well if you do as I say.*"

All this time, Mesmeranza had been sitting bolt upright, mouthing the words along with Miss Fly and adding her own gestures. Miss Fly paused to mop her nose.

"Go on," snapped Mesmeranza. "Get to the best bit."

"I am, I am. *Tonight, on the stroke of midnight, you will rise and go down to the kitchen. As you are doubtless aware, there is a loose flagstone directly before the hearth, under the rug. Beneath is a large book. It belonged to Grandmother and is rightfully mine, no matter what Demelza may have told you. On no account must you open it. It is also advised that you wear gloves. You will bring it to the large oak tree where the path divides. I shall be waiting. You will tell no one of this. One word to my sister and all bets are off. Burn this letter as soon as you have read it. My instructions must be obeyed or it will be the worst for your brother.*"

68

Miss Fly reached the end. There was a pause.

"So what do you think?" asked Mesmeranza.

"I've told you what I think," sniffed Miss Fly. "I think it's despicable. Kidnap, blackmail, betrayal, theft, greed, revenge—it's got everything."

"I know," said Mesmeranza smugly. "All very satisfying. The perfect Plan. This time, nobody shall thwart me. I'm unthwartable."

"What about young Wilf? The boy who—"

"I know who you mean, Fly, you don't have to spell it out. Master Brownswoody will have nothing to do with this. I'm keeping him very busy at the moment, delivering boxes of groceries to far-flung addresses. He doesn't have time to breathe."

"And that's it?" said Miss Fly.

"That's it. I get Grandmother's Bad Spell Book and Demelza gets her just deserts. And Clover Twig finally learns the consequences of daring to cross me."

"You really are ruthless, aren't you?" said Miss Fly.

"Why, thank you, Fly. I'll take that as a compliment. Now, go and write it up on the letterhead paper in your best writing. Bring it to me for signing. Don't forget to enclose a snippet of that disgusting rag. Knowing practical little Miss Twig, she'll want proof."

"All right." Miss Fly sighed, gathered up her pencil

and pad, and stood up. Her nose was blocked, her head was beginning to throb, and she wanted to get away.

"Find a first-class stamp. I want it posted first thing in the morning so that it arrives the following day. Mark it PRIVATE and URGENT."

"But what if your sister sees it?"

"She won't. The girl is always up first in the mornings, doing chores. She collects the mail. Go on, then, don't hang around. Oh, before you do, go down to the kitchens and tell Mrs. Chunk I'm ready for my supper tray."

"All right," said Miss Fly miserably. She had to go down anyway, to collect the cats' supper bucket.

★ ★ ★ ★ ★

The kitchens were situated in the lower part of the castle. They were presided over by Mrs. Chunk, who, as well as being an excellent cook, happened to be the proud mother of the castle jailer. Her son was called Humperdump—a large, clunking name that suited him very nicely.

Humperdump's territory was the dungeons, which were a level down from the kitchens, reached by a stone staircase behind a studded door situated next to the broom cupboard. This was very convenient, as Humperdump was a big eater and usually ate his meals at the kitchen table, leaving Jimbo Squint, his right-hand man, to guard the prisoners. Right now, there were no prisoners, so both of them hung around the kitchens a lot, hoping for a hot biscuit or a slice of cake, which was never long in coming.

Miss Fly, pencil stuck behind her ear and pad in her cardigan pocket, came slapping down the steps and paused uneasily at the kitchen door. Was he in there? She hoped not. Miss Fly dreaded bumping into Humperdump Chunk. Some time ago, much to her horror, he had bizarrely decided to fall in love with her. She certainly hadn't encouraged his advances. She had ripped up his love notes, screamed in his face, and, at one point, stomped on his foot. Thankfully, he had finally gotten the message, but now she had to put up with his injured sniffs and hurt glances.

His mum wasn't so friendly these days, either. Whenever Miss Fly made her daily trip down to the kitchens to collect fish heads for the cats, the bucket was handed over in strained silence. And her breakfast toast was always burned, she noticed.

Miss Fly opened the door and sidled in. To her relief, there was no sign of Humperdump. Mrs. Chunk was standing next to the big stove, stirring something in a pot while the kitchen maids clattered around doing kitcheny things. Jimbo Squint stood leaning against a wall, eating a large slice of pie.

Mrs. Chunk noticed Miss Fly skulking and pointed in stony silence to the bucket in the corner. Miss Fly tiptoed over and picked it up.

"Thank you," she said humbly. Mrs. Chunk stirred and said nothing.

"Evenin', Miss Fly," said Jimbo Squint, with a leer.

"Good evening, Squint," said Miss Fly shortly. She wasn't keen on Jimbo, either. She was just about to scuttle away when she remembered. "Oh, Mrs. Chunk . . . her ladyship would like her tray now, if you please."

Mrs. Chunk tightened her lips and gave the briefest of nods. No more was forthcoming, so Miss Fly retreated and began the long climb back up to her apartment. She was looking forward to getting the cats fed, then sitting in her hairy armchair. She needed to do some serious thinking.

CHAPTER SIX

Two Unexpected Meetings

I can't believe we've lost him, thought Clover as she hurried along the track leading to Mrs. Eckles's cottage. *How could we lose him? How?*

It had been the most awful day of her life—and it still wasn't over. It was like a bad dream. Hour after hour, tramping through the woods, fighting down panic, calling and calling—and all for nothing. Herby was lost.

And now it was dark. The last glimmers of orange light were gone. Even if there had been a moon, which there wasn't, it wouldn't have penetrated down here, below the trees. The faint light of her lantern made little impression on the surrounding night. If anything, it made the shadows even deeper. It was lucky the track was so familiar, as she could hardly see her feet. Even so, she automatically kept peering into the bushes, hoping to see a familiar little shape. Once, she had tried calling his name—but only once. Her voice sounded too lonely, out here in the darkness.

A short way behind her, there came the crack of a twig followed by the sound of a sharp intake of breath as something—or somebody—collided with a tree. Clover stopped in her tracks and whirled around, heart leaping with hope.

"*Ow!*" exclaimed a familiar voice. "*Darn* it!"

Oh.

"Wilf?" called Clover. "Where are you?"

"Clover? Is that you?"

"Of course it's me. I'm over here. Can't you see the lantern?"

There came the sound of footsteps and Wilf came limping into the small pool of light, rubbing his head.

"What are you doing here?" he asked in surprise. "I thought you'd have been back hours ago."

"I would have been," said Clover. "But something awful has happened. You see . . ."

And she told him everything.

"Oh my," said Wilf, when she finally reached the end. "So Herby's lost. That's not good."

"I know. I don't suppose you've seen any signs?"

"'Fraid not. Of course, I wasn't looking. I thought I heard people shouting a while back, but I didn't know what it was about. *Ouch.*"

"What?" said Clover.

"Blisters. Feels like I've walked halfway around the world today. Three deliveries, and all of them were out. Mrs. Pluck gave me an earful too. I really hate this job. Grampy'll have a right moan, with me getting back so late. Ow, my feet really *hurt.*"

"Stuff your boots with moss," sighed Clover. "And tie up the laces. They're dangling all over. Hurry up, I've got to see Mrs. Eckles."

"All right," said Wilf, collapsing onto a handy nearby stump. "Hold up the lantern so I can see what I'm doing." He bent forward to deal with his laces, then said, slowly, "Hello. What's this?"

There, lying on the ground among the moss and twigs, was a small scrap of red rag.

They both stared at it. Slowly, Clover stooped and picked it up.

"It's a piece of his rag," she said. "He's been here. Oh, Wilf, he was *here!*"

"He was," said a grim voice from behind, making them both jump. "But he ain't here now."

"Mrs. Eckles!" gasped Clover, as the familiar figure emerged from the shadows. "What are you doing here?"

"Comin' to find you. You're late. Thought I told you to be back by sundown."

"Yes, but—"

"All right, all right, I know you got a good reason. I know Herby's gone missin'."

"I suppose you saw that in the stars," said Wilf. "Using your mystic powers."

"Nope, yer grampy told me. He came bangin' on my door. Knew it was somethin' serious for him to come a-callin'. Asked if I'd heard. Said if I saw you to tell you he's gone out lookin' with a search party from the Axes. No point, they won't find 'im. He's a long way from the woods by now. A *long* way. If you get my meanin'."

She turned her green eyes on Clover.

"Oh," said Clover. Her heart turned a somersault. "You don't mean . . ."

"I do. He's taken the Perilous Path."

"But you don't *know* that!" cried Clover. "He might be hiding or asleep or . . ." Her voice trailed off.

"I saw him," said Mrs. Eckles. "The Path was there, not more than ten minutes ago. But it ain't there now. Been and gone. It was already fadin' when I arrived. Saw the glow, went as quick as I could, but just missed it. I could see it had been pullin' out all the stops, though. Makin' itself look pretty. Fairy lights on the bridge, star shine on the water."

"But you saw Herby?"

"Halfway across. Sack with a red pocket, right? And that new red hat you knitted. Fadin' away. Then gone."

Clover looked down. She didn't trust herself to speak.

"If it's any consolation, there was no sign of Old Barry," added Mrs. Eckles.

At this point, Wilf considered butting in but saw Clover's face and kept quiet.

"So now you know," said Mrs. Eckles. "Question is, 'ow to get 'im back."

"You can do it, can't you?" asked Clover, suddenly hopeful. "Get him back?"

"What, just twiddle me fingers and wait for 'im to fall outta the sky?" Mrs. Eckles shook her head. "It don't work like that. The Path's got 'im now. It don't take kindly to interference."

"But he's only a *baby*!"

"I know. Easy pickin's."

Clover swallowed hard. She didn't trust herself to speak.

"Hey," mumbled Wilf kindly. "It's all right. You can cry if you like. Can't she, Mrs. Eckles?"

"I'm not *crying*."

"She can," said Mrs. Eckles briskly, "if she wants to waste time. Come on now, Clover, shape up. You'll need your wits about you if you're goin' in after him. Hate to say it, but it's the only way. You up for it?"

"Of course I'm going after him," said Clover. To her relief, her voice was steady.

"*We*, you mean," said Wilf. "We're all going, aren't we, Mrs. Eckles? We'll catch up to him in no time." There was a little silence. He looked from one to the other. "What?"

"I'll do what I can to help," said Mrs. Eckles. "But I can't come with you. Witches don't walk the Perilous Path. It changes us. Brings out the nasty side."

"Oh. Right," said Wilf. He didn't want to see Mrs. Eckles's nasty side. Even her nice side wasn't that great. "It's all down to you and me then, Clover."

"Just me," said Clover. "He's my brother."

"Try going without me," said Wilf stoutly.

"Of course he's goin'," said Mrs. Eckles briskly.

"You'll need all the backup you can get. A hero would be better, of course, but Wilf'll have to do."

"You see?" said Wilf. "You're stuck with me. Anyway, I want to find Herby as much as you do." He turned to Mrs. Eckles. "So, tell me about this Path. What sort of perils are we talking about?"

"Can't tell you," said Mrs. Eckles. "Folks don't often come back to tell—and those that do don't say much. Just remember that peril comes in all forms, some of 'em quite surprisin'. They ain't all obvious, like Old Barry."

"Who's Old Barry?"

"The Troll," explained Clover impatiently. "I told you about him."

"Don't be put off," Mrs. Eckles went on. "Remember, he can't leave the bridge, so he's limited. Once you've answered the questions, he has to let you pass. Although just to be on the safe side, I wouldn't turn yer back on 'im."

"Right," said Wilf. "Don't turn your back on Old Barry. Right. What questions?"

"Clover knows."

"I do," said Clover. "You can leave that bit to me."

"Don't eat nothin' on the Path," continued Mrs. Eckles. "Don't pick berries, especially red ones. Be wary of drinkin' the water. Avoid goin' inside anywhere, like strange buildin's or caves. Things ain't always what they seem, so don't get taken in. Oh—here. Coupla things."

She rummaged in her pocket. Wilf gave Clover a nudge. Up to now, Mrs. Eckles's advice had been a dreary list of don'ts. The sort of thing that grown-ups always said to little kids the first time they went out alone. He was hoping for a magic potion or a protective device or something exciting and useful.

What Mrs. Eckles produced was none of those.

"Oh," said Clover, surprised. "My mirror. I don't think I'll have time for my hair."

She reached out and took it. Her own small, cracked hand mirror that she had shared with the girls until going to live with Mrs. Eckles. She had pinched it for herself, knowing that they would only break it. It seemed a silly thing to bring.

"Ah, but reflective surfaces come in handy when you're receivin'," said Mrs. Eckles.

"Receiving? Receiving what?"

"Me, of course, who d'you think? I'll be staying in touch, won't I? I can't be there in the flesh, but I can give you the benefit of me wisdom. I'll borrow Ida's fancy new Crystal Ball. Can't be that hard to get me

head 'round. I won't guarantee a great reception, mind. The Path won't like bein' spied on. But the mirror should help. Stick it in yer basket. If it starts to hum, that's me. Answer quick, 'cause I might be cut off."

"Anything else?" asked Wilf hopefully.

"Like what?"

"Well, you know. A bottle of Changeme Potion? Or some Invisibility Pills? Or—um—a magic sword?"

"Ah, you don't need any o' that." Mrs. Eckles flapped her hand dismissively. "Magic just complicates things. You'd slice yer feet off with a magic sword, I know you."

"I'd be *careful*. I just meant for an emergency."

"Nope." Mrs. Eckles shook her head. "The Path won't like it. Just keep a clear head and make good decisions. And if you want a bit more advice, don't waste time fightin' if there's an option to run. Remember what you're there for. In and out, quick as you can."

"So how do we get back? Once we've found Herby?" asked Clover.

"I'll 'ave to think about that. Leave it to me, and I'll let you know when the time comes."

"But what if we get into *real* trouble?" insisted Wilf. "Like, what if there are—I dunno—fire-breathing dragons or bug-eyed monsters? A weapon'd come in handy, wouldn't it? "

"You can't beat a good, stout stick," said Mrs. Eckles. "There's one right there, look by your foot."

"I always end up with just a stick," complained Wilf. "I ended up with just a stick the last time something like this happened."

"Stop complaining and pick it up," said Clover.

Wilf picked it up. He waved it about a bit. Just the right size and length. It felt good in his hand. He would stick with a stick. "Right," he said. "I'm ready. Now what?"

"Now you start walkin'," said Mrs. Eckles.

"Where to?"

"Anywhere you like. It don't matter which direction you take, the Path'll find you. It knows you're lookin'."

"It does?" Clover glanced around into the surrounding trees and suppressed a little shiver.

"Oh, yes. It'll seek you out. Anyway, I'm off 'ome to collect the broomstick. Then I'll go to Ida's to borrow the Ball. You'll be hearin' from me, soon as I can. All this newfangled technology, it ain't me. But never say I ain't up to a challenge. Oh—one last thing."

She took a small, wrapped package from her pocket, dropped it into Wilf's hand, then abruptly turned on her heel and walked off.

"What's in it?" shouted Wilf as her footsteps receded.

"Cheese sandwiches," came the reply. It already came from a long way off. "Don't eat 'em all at once!"

"She's right," said Clover firmly. "*I'll* take those." She took the package and popped it into her basket.

"Aren't you going to wish us good luck?" called Wilf.

"No such thing!" came the faint response "You makes yer own luck."

"See?" said Clover. "*I* told you that."

They stood in the guttering light of the lantern. All around them, the night pressed in. Now that Mrs. Eckles had gone, it suddenly seemed—unsafe.

"Right," said Wilf. "I suppose we should start walking. Which way, do you th—?" He broke off as Clover gave him a sudden, sharp dig in the ribs. "*Ouch*. What?"

"Sssh. Listen. Don't you hear it? Running water. Over to the left, I think."

Clover held up the lantern. Its light was even fainter now. It was running out of oil.

"You're right," said Wilf. He peered into the dense foliage. "There's a space between the thorn bushes. A little gap. See it?"

"I see it. I'll go first."

"No, I will. I've got the stick."

"No," said Clover firmly. "You bring up the rear."

"Why? Look, I think we should talk about this. Why is it always you—"

Suddenly, Wilf was yanked off his feet. They plunged off the trail and into the darkness, just as the lantern went out.

CHAPTER SEVEN

Old Barry

It happened really quickly and unexpectedly. A minute or two of blundering blindly through thorny undergrowth—and suddenly, there it was.

A small wooden bridge spanning a river. Thick green fog swirled over and around the bridge, blocking out the far end. The dark water beneath flowed along sluggishly. It smelled brackish.

"It doesn't look very alluring, does it?" whispered Clover. "I thought there would be silvery lights."

"It's the second show tonight, remember? It pulled out all the stops for Herby," said Wilf. "It's probably tired. At least there's no sign of a Troll—"

"I'S A-COMIN' TO GETCHA!"

The sudden roar came from the darkness under the bridge. There was a horrible sucking, bubbling noise, and a large, dripping shape came wading from the shadows. Froglike, it leaped up onto the bank and stood in a low crouch, knuckles brushing the ground.

"Oops," said Clover. "Spoke too soon. Leave this to me, all right?"

Old Barry was dressed in a filthy vest and ragged trousers held up by a belt with a buckle shaped like a fish bone. A matching set of smaller bones dangled from his scaly ears. He had bloodshot eyes and a mouth full of broken teeth. Thick mud oozed down his long arms and dripped off the ends of his horny fingernails. To complete the vision of loveliness, there was indeed a small tree growing out of his forehead.

Mrs. Eckles was right. Old Barry was *really* ugly. Clover hoped she had been right about him not being allowed to leave the bridge. She took a deep breath—and engaged.

"I don't want to be rude," she said, "but can we skip the roaring?"

"Eh?" said Old Barry.

"The roaring. And all the stuff about *getting us*, whatever that means. Can we move on? We're in a hurry. I'd like to get straight to the questions."

Wilf was impressed. If Clover was scared, she certainly wasn't showing it. His first instinct on seeing his first-ever Troll had been to run away screaming. He swished his stick around a bit, just to show that the thought had never crossed his mind.

"Just somethin' I do," said Old Barry, scowling.

"Well, you shouldn't."

"You're supposed to be scared."

"Well, we're not. Questions, please."

"All right, all right. There's three."

"Yes, I know. Three questions."

"No," said Barry firmly. "*Questions Three*."

"Whatever. Just get on with it."

Barry straightened and licked his blubbery lips. This was clearly his big moment.

"Question the First: *What is my name?*"

"Old Barry."

"Oh—bum!" Old Barry was exceedingly put out. "Who told you that?"

"Is that the second question?" inquired Clover.

"Eh? Oh—no."

"Well, what is then?"

"Question the Second: *What*," said Old Barry with a cunning air, "*is my favorite color?*"

"Brown."

"Look," said Old Barry, "you been talking to someone, aincha?"

"It's common knowledge, Barry. And before you ask, you had fish for breakfast. You should try varying the questions a bit."

"They is *good* questions," snarled Old Barry. "Nothing wrong with my questions."

"She's right, though. Some new ones would make a change," observed Wilf.

"But I won't know the *answers*, will I? I knows the *answers* to these!"

"So do we, so you've got to let us pass," said Clover. "But first, I've got a question of my own. Has a little boy passed this way?"

"Don't have to answer that," said Old Barry sulkily.

"Come on, Barry, be nice for once. He's a very little boy. My brother. Not much more than a baby. I'm just asking if you've seen him."

"Dunno," said Old Barry. He gave a shrug. "Somefin'

91

did come trip-trip-trappin' over the bridge a while back, but it sounded too small to bovver wiv. A rabbit or somefin'."

"You didn't bother to check?"

"I was on a fish break. Gotta eat sometime."

Clover and Wilf stared at each other.

"That's him," said Wilf. "Come on, let's go. Stand back, Barry. We're coming over."

"A please'd be nice," said Old Barry sulkily. But he loped back down the bank and stood with his huge hands dangling, giving them surly looks.

"I'll go first," said Wilf, grabbing Clover's arm. "I've got the stick."

"No," said Clover firmly. She shook his hand off. "Me first. Wait 'til I get over and guard my back, just in case Barry gets any ideas. Then follow on."

And with no more ado, she stepped toward the bridge and disappeared into the green fog.

Wilf gave a sigh. She could be very bossy sometimes. He took a firm hold of his stick and turned back to Barry.

"You can stop all that," said Barry. "All that with the stick. I ain't doin' nothin'."

Wilf considered for a moment, then lowered the stick.

"Fair enough," he said. "But I've got my eye on you."

An awkward little silence fell. Wilf felt he needed to fill it in.

"So," he said. "What's with the fish thing? Is that all you eat?"

"Mostly."

"I see you've got a sort of fish *theme* going on there, with the buckle and earrings."

"So? I likes fish."

"So it's fish for breakfast and fish for lunch, is it?"

"Nothin' wrong with that."

"Well, no. Good for the brain, aren't they? Fish? Make you come up with really good questions to ask."

Barry glared up at him from the bank and growled, "They *was* good questions."

"No, they weren't," said Wilf. "A good question is how long is a piece of string? Or why can't you tickle yourself? Or why are there wasps?"

Old Barry stared at him.

"Ah, shut up," he said eventually. "I've 'ad enough of you. Find yer own way over, see if I care."

There was a splash, a swirl of bubbles—and he was gone.

"And good riddance to you too," said Wilf with a grin, and turned to face the bridge. One Troll down. Not a bad start. Slowly, the grin dissolved.

The swirling, sickly green fog seemed to have inten-
sified. It seemed to have—it almost seemed to have
shapes in it. Horrible, ever-changing shapes with horns
and mouths and teeth. At one point, he thought he
could make out a giant frog, which slowly transformed
into something that looked like a cross between a
vulture and a lizard. It hurt his eyes to look.

"Clover?" he shouted. His own voice sounded muffled to his ears. For a long, agonizing moment, there
was silence. Then . . .

"Wilf? I'm over. Come on, what are you waiting for?"

Her voice sounded strangely distant.

"Coming!" he shouted. And he moved forward and
stepped into the fog and onto the bridge.

Instantly, his head began to swim.

Wilf wasn't good with heights. He hated crossing
bridges, especially slatted ones. Heights made his legs
turn to jelly and his stomach flip over. And yet he always
had a terrible compulsion to look down.

Green fog swirled around him as he stepped onto
the first creaking slat. The fog was in his eyes and ears
and up his nose. It smelled . . . rotten. It reminded him
of wormy apples and old mushrooms. His skin had a
nasty tingling sensation, as though a thousand little
fingers were pinching him.

His left boot went down the gap between the first and second slat and he stumbled, nearly dropping his stick.

"Close your eyes," came Clover's faint voice. It sounded even farther away and had a strange echo. "Hold the handrail and feel your way across. It's only a few steps."

"I'm coming," ground out Wilf. "Just give me a minute, I can't see a thing."

"But I can see you. It's clear over here. It's no distance at all. Walk straight ahead with your eyes closed."

Wilf closed his eyes. If it was only a few steps, how come she sounded so far away?

Firmly gripping the rail, he willed himself to shuffle forward. One step—two—three—four—five—

"That's it," came Clover's voice. "You're halfway. Just don't look down."

Oh dear. That fatal urge to look down when somebody tells you not to.

Wilf couldn't help it. He opened his eyes—just a fraction—and looked down.

And down.

And down!

Oh, horror! He wasn't on a little wooden bridge at all! He was on a flimsy rope bridge, swaying vertiginously across a ravine that ended far, far below in a raging river that frothed and foamed over razor-sharp rocks!

"Ahhhh!" wailed Wilf. He staggered, and the rope bridge wobbled horribly.

"Close your eyes!" came Clover's voice. "It's not real, Wilf! *It's not real!*"

But, oh my goodness, it certainly felt real. His knees were beginning to buckle; he could feel them giving way. The bridge was swaying—wobbling—he was losing his balance—

. . . *he was falling!*

CHAPTER EIGHT

Mrs. Eckles Borrows the Ball

Granny Dismal was awoken by a furious banging on her front door—despite the woolly nightcap and the cotton wool stuffed in her ears. And the dozen blankets and eiderdowns she always slept beneath, being a chilly sort of soul.

"Ida?" came the shrill cry from outside. "Open up, this is an emergency!"

Whatever did Demelza Eckles want at this time of night?

Granny Dismal felt torn. She'd been on the Ball all evening, breaking the news about the reappearance of the Perilous Path to her fellow Witches. The reactions had been varied. One or two had heard already, which was disappointing. Some wanted details. But most had gone very quiet, thanked her for the warning, and cut the connection. All in all, she had made nine calls, which was tiring both to the eyes and throat. She needed her sleep.

But then again, emergencies didn't come her way too often.

"Ida!" came the urgent cry. There was more banging. "Did you hear what I said? It's bad news."

Bad news? Ah, that sealed it. Granny Dismal hesitated no more. She heaved herself out of bed, stuffed her feet into her slippers, and reached for her collection of dressing gowns.

★ ★ ★ ★ ★

Outside, Mrs. Eckles paced up and down, occasionally pausing to rub her aching rear. She rarely used the broomstick these days. It was too uncomfortable. It chafed her thighs, even with the extra pair of padded undies. Besides, she didn't like drawing attention to herself. A talking gate was one thing, but a flying broomstick was unnecessarily flashy. These days, it mostly got used by Clover for sweeping. But you couldn't beat a broomstick if it was speed you were after. Right now, it was propped next to the drainpipe, faintly pulsing with whatever is the wooden equivalent of adrenaline.

After what seemed like an age, the door opened and Granny Dismal peered out, wearing the nightcap, the slippers, three dressing gowns, and a couple of scarves for added safety.

"What bad news?" she said.

"I need to borrow your new Crystal," said Mrs. Eckles.

"Oh, really?" said Granny Dismal. "Thought you didn't approve of them. What bad news?"

"Herby Twig's gone missing. Taken the Perilous Path. Clover's gone after him, with Wilf Brownswoody. I need to get in touch."

"So it's all different now, then," said Granny Dismal.

"Yes! Look, come on, Ida, I don't 'ave time for this."

Mrs. Eckles was hopping from foot to foot, wringing her hands with anxiety. Granny Dismal let her hop and wring a bit more, just for the pleasure of seeing her do it, then finally relented.

"All right," she said. "You'd better come in."

"No, I'm not stopping. Just pass it over and I'll be off."

"It's not as simple as that. It's a very advanced piece of equipment."

"Don't it come with instructions?"

"You wouldn't understand them."

"Ah, come on, how hard can it be?"

"Ball gazing's an art," said Granny Dismal. "You can cause a lot of damage. I'm not letting it out of my sight unless I'm confident you know what you're doing. It's pre-programmed with all my important data."

"Yer what?"

"See what I mean? You don't even know the basics. You need intensive instruction."

"Oh, all *right*," Mrs. Eckles said with a sigh. "But get a move on, eh?"

Once inside, Granny Dismal waddled around lighting lamps that did little to cheer up the kitchen, which was bleak, gray, and chilly, just like her. Mrs. Eckles fumed and fretted, wishing she could plant her boot up Granny Dismal's backside.

Finally, when the lamps were all lit to her satisfaction, Granny Dismal reached deep into her many layers and, after some rummaging, produced a key.

"It's in my private cupboard," she announced pointedly, and waited.

Mrs. Eckles respectfully turned her back. All Witches have private cupboards. It isn't considered good form to look inside. The contents are highly secret and jealously guarded. She heard a door click open, then firmly close again.

"All right," said Granny Dismal. "You can look now."

On the kitchen table was a round glass object, about the size of a melon. It appeared to be empty apart from a ghostly wisp of curling gray mist, which drifted about, gently bumping into the curved sides. The Crystal was set atop a shiny black square base, on which was mounted a bewildering array of tiny buttons, switches, and levers. Above one of the buttons, a small red light blinked on and off. Lying beside it on the table was a velvet carrying bag with a drawstring.

"That's it?" said Mrs. Eckles. She moved closer and peered down.

"That's it," said Granny Dismal proudly. The Ballmaster Mark Six. Best there is."

"So it'll tune into the Path?"

"It's multidimensional," said Granny Dismal. "So it should. But I've never tested it out. There's some places I don't go."

"Wise," said Mrs. Eckles, and they both nodded.

"Tricky lookin', ain't it?" remarked Mrs. Eckles. "Don't look like any Ball I've seen."

"How many have you seen?"

"One," admitted Mrs. Eckles. "Grandmother's. My sister's got that."

"Well, there you are," said Granny Dismal dismissively. "Ball technology's advanced a lot since then."

"It's certainly gotten more complicated." Mrs. Eckles reached out an experimental finger.

"Don't touch it!" snapped Granny Dismal. "It's *booting up*. Finding its power. You mustn't touch it until the red light goes out."

"What would happen if I did?"

"It might crash. You could cause a short."

"How long does it take to do that thing? What you said?"

"Boot up? Two to three minutes."

"If *I* give it a boot, would that make it work quicker?"

"Are you being funny?"

"It works with my gate. Let's 'ave a look at the instructions, then, while we're waitin'."

Granny Dismal reached inside the velvet bag, produced a printed booklet, and passed it to Mrs. Eckles.

"You won't make sense of it," she warned. "I'll have to take you through the whole procedure, step by step."

"How long's that gonna take?"

"Take a while," said Granny Dismal, clearly relishing her role as expert. "First, I have to explain about the signal. You have to position the Ball right or it scrambles. And you have to do things in the right order. *Don't touch that button!*" Mrs. Eckles had her experimental finger out again, but Granny Dismal was ready for her and smacked it away. "What did I say? Do that again and you don't get to borrow it, emergency or no emergency."

"Sorry," said Mrs. Eckles humbly. She took a respectful step backward. "All right, I'll listen. Sorry."

"You'll need to take notes. You can use my shopping list pad; you can replace it later. I have to go upstairs and get my reading glasses. For the small print."

"All right," said Mrs. Eckles. "You do that, Ida."

Granny Dismal shuffled off. Mrs. Eckles waited until she heard the stairs creak, then leaped into action. She cast around for the shopping list pad. There it was, hanging on the pantry door. A slim, gray, floating pen hovered conveniently above it. She plucked the pen from the air and scribbled on the top sheet. It didn't work. With a cross exclamation, Mrs. Eckles chucked it away. The pen calmly floated back to its original position in the vain hope that its floatiness would compensate for its lack of inkiness.

Luckily, the list came equipped with a backup pencil stub, so she reached for that.

Behind her, the red light winked out. From somewhere in the black base, there started up a low, gentle humming sound, like bees in a hive, and the wisp of gray mist expanded until it filled the Crystal. Apparently, the Ball had—what was it again? Got its boots on.

When Granny Dismal finally descended from above, reading glasses in hand, there was an empty space where the Ballmaster Mark Six had been, a missing carrying bag, a missing instruction manual, a wide open front door, and a brief note on the shopping list pad. The note said:

dont wory ill figger it out. spred the word.

Granny Dismal wasn't very happy.

★ ★ ★ ★ ★

Neville opened a sleepy eye as his mistress came crashing into the cottage, windblown, red in the face, and towing the broomstick behind her. In her hand was a black velvet bag, which was emitting a shrill, urgent beeping noise.

BEEP! BEEP! BEEEEEEEEEEP!

"It's beepin'!" cried Mrs. Eckles, chucking the bag on the kitchen table as though it were burning her fingers. "It's beepin' at me, Nev! All the way 'ome! Why's it beepin'?"

Neville didn't know, of course. He was a cat.

He stared curiously at the beeping bag. Clearly not edible, which was a shame. But there was no way he was getting back to sleep with that racket going on. Perhaps he would kill it.

Putting it like that makes it sound as though Neville can think properly. He can't. His thoughts are mostly just a confused series of big question marks, like this: ?????. . . . ????. . . . ????????. . . . . ?

Feigning disinterest, he stood, stretched, sauntered over to the table, leaped up, and eyed the beeping bag, which showed no signs of shutting up.

"Nev!" shouted Mrs. Eckles. "Get down, you silly! You might cause a long. I mean, a short!"

But the warning was lost on Neville. He was only a cat. He touched the bag with his nose.

The shrill beeping suddenly changed to a continuous,

ear-splitting screech. Neville's ears flattened and he backed away, hissing.

EEEEEEEEEEEEEEEEEEEEEEEEEEEEEEEE . . .

"Oh, my!" cried Mrs. Eckles, clapping her hands over her ears. "*Now* see, you naughty!"

EEEEEEEEEEEEEEEEEEEEEEEEEEEEEEE . . .

"How do we stop it? Get out of the way, let me . . . ouch, it's hot! . . . It's gonna blow. Get back, Nev, it's gonna blow . . ."

EEEEEEEEEEEEEEEEEEEEEEEEEEEEEEEEE . . .

That's when Mrs. Eckles used the frying pan.

CHAPTER NINE

On the Path

Wilf lay on a grassy bank with his eyes screwed shut.

"You can get up now," said Clover.

"'S'all right," croaked Wilf. "I'm fine where I am." He could hardly get the words out, his mouth was so dry.

He found it hard to believe he was still alive and

kicking. He had actually been *falling*—before Clover's hand had emerged from the fog, gripped his shoulder, and briskly yanked him back from certain death. Just in the nick of time. *Phew!*

Feebly, he groped around for his stick. His right hand closed on it. At least he hadn't lost that.

"Look, I know you had a scare," said Clover, "but you're all right now. Stop messing about and sit up."

Reflecting that Clover would make a terrible nurse, Wilf eased himself into a sitting position. He still couldn't open his eyes, though. He clutched his wobbling stomach and groaned.

"You're making an awful fuss," said Clover. "All this for just crossing a little bridge."

"There were rocks," protested Wilf piteously. "Rocks and a river, and I was miles up on a rope bri—"

"No, you weren't. You just thought you were. You were fine at first, when you closed your eyes like I told you. Then you went all doddery and started tottering about. Then you decided to hurl yourself over the rail. You were just wasting time."

"But the fog! That horrible green fog with a frog in it . . ."

"There isn't any fog or frogs. In fact, there isn't any bridge. Look, if you don't believe me."

Wilf opened his eyes and looked around. Then he rubbed them and looked again. Clover was right. There was no fog—and the bridge had vanished, together with the river. Now there was nothing but trees. Trees and thick, tangled bushes. It was as though the forest had closed up behind them.

Before them was a path. A simple dirt trail leading off straight ahead. It began at the grass verge, right at their feet.

"Notice something?" said Clover.

"What?"

"It's light."

It was, too. Shafts of bright yellow sunlight fell across the path. Too bright. Unnaturally bright. In fact, everything seemed unnatural. The trees were too close together. The shadows behind them were too—shadowy. The grass they sat on was too green. There were no birds singing. Just silence, and the Path leading into the woods. It didn't look exactly *perilous*. Rather lovely, in a way, leading off into sharp, cool greenness. But things didn't feel right.

"Odd, isn't it?" said Clover. She put out a hand into a patch of sunlight. There was no warmth in it. "It's all too bright. It's like—almost pretend. Like it's covering up something else. Something—I don't know.

Something darker. Something—else." She suppressed a little shiver.

"I know," agreed Wilf, staring around. "Weird about the daylight. It looks like time's different here. When we get home, we'll probably find that years have gone by and nobody will remember us." Clover gave a little frown, and he added, "Only joking. Can I have a sandwich? Before we get cracking? To keep my strength up?"

"Don't you ever think about anything else but food?" sighed Clover. Although, come to think of it, she hadn't eaten anything since breakfast. Just a small bowl of porridge, because she had wanted to get away early. It seemed a long, long time ago, when everything was normal. Well, as normal as usual. Clover sometimes felt that she was the only sensible one in a crazy world.

She took out the package and unwrapped the sandwiches. They were typical of Mrs. Eckles, who was very hit-and-miss in the kitchen. The bread was unevenly sliced and the cheese was last week's leftovers. She had forgotten the butter and hadn't bothered to cut the crusts off. And she had made only three. But they were cheese sandwiches, and right now they would do just fine.

Clover broke the top one in two and handed half to Wilf.

"Here. We'll share one. But no more. These are all we've got."

They bit into them and sat chewing in silence, staring at the Path. There was no doubt about it. It was too straight. No natural path was as straight as that.

"I don't expect Herby noticed the weirdness," said Clover. She hoped what she was saying was true. "He's just a baby. He hasn't learned about nasty things yet."

"What about his rag? If that's not nasty, I don't know what is."

"True." Clover gave a little sigh. "He knows about poisonous toadstools, too. And the girls are mean to him sometimes. They didn't give him his fair share of sweets. That's how it all started. They won't admit it, but I know them."

"That's mean," agreed Wilf, who had finished his bit of sandwich in two bites. "Not sharing. Do you want all your bit of sandwich?"

"Yes. So he took the bag and went off with them and got lost and now he's . . ." Her eyes went to the Path. She trailed off and bit her lip.

"He'll be all right," said Wilf. "We'll catch up with him in no time. He's lucky, he's got all the sweets. Did I tell you about the one you gave me? It was fantastic.

Like fizzy fruit cake mixed with cherries. And . . . I dunno. Sunsets or something. I wish I had one now."

"There are no birds, have you noticed?" said Clover.

Wilf listened. And then, suddenly, somewhere overhead, right on cue, a bird began singing. It sounded like a blackbird, but even better. It trilled and soared and warbled. The song was wonderful.

But then—it choked. It choked, and an evil-sounding, cawing rasp came out. It was hard to describe, that rasp, but it certainly shouldn't have come from a blackbird's throat. There was a moment's hesitation, then the song began again, even lovelier than before.

They looked at each other.

"Anything else in your basket?" asked Wilf hopefully. "I mean, anything that we might use as a weapon? As well as my stick? Like—I dunno—your pin cushion?"

"What, so we can prick our way out of danger, you mean?" scoffed Clover, adding, "Anyway, I don't have it. It's empty. Just the sandwiches and the mirror, that's all."

She didn't mention that there was a loose sweet rolling around in the bottom. Somehow, it had accidentally fallen out of the paper bag. It was a blue one. For all her good intentions, Clover had finally given in to curiosity and saved it for herself, for later. Just the one. She didn't want to be greedy.

"Anything in your pockets?" asked Wilf. Clover checked.

"Just my hanky."

"So that's it, then. Two cheese sandwiches, a mirror, a stick, and your hanky. That's the sum total of our equipment."

"It is," Clover said, sighing. "But it's all we've got. Come on, let's go. The longer we are here, the farther away Herby gets."

They brushed off the crumbs and stood up. Side by side they stepped down onto the Perilous Path. And began walking.

* * ★ * *

To begin with, the Path went straight, as though someone had measured it with a ruler. It cut directly through the tall, overhanging trees. Everything was very still. Even the lone blackbird—if that's what it was—seemed to have flown away.

"Clover?" muttered Wilf uneasily.

"What?"

"This is weird. I keep getting the feeling we're being watched."

Clover said nothing. Her eyes were fixed to the ground, which consisted of hard-packed mud and clumps of short, tough, bright green grass that showed no sign of small passing footprints.

"Clover?"

"What?"

"I've just noticed something. My blisters don't hurt. I was in agony before. Now I'm fine. I haven't had any accidents, either, not since the bridge. Maybe the Path likes us. Or me, at any rate. "

"More likely it's keen to hurry us along," said Clover. "We'd never get anywhere with you falling over and leaping off bridges."

She sounded quite snappy. But then, she was worried about Herby. Wilf decided to let it pass.

"How much longer, do you think?" he asked. "Before we get somewhere? Do we just tramp endlessly through weird woods in a straight line?"

"I don't know, do I? Stop jabbering and look for clues."

"I *am*. I just wish . . ." He broke off. "Clover?"

"What *now*? Just keep your eyes on the ground."

"Never mind the ground," said Wilf. He pointed. "Look."

Up ahead, there was something in the Path. A wooden signpost. It stood at a crossroads, its arms pointing in four directions.

"Was that there just now?" asked Wilf. "If so, I didn't notice."

"Me neither," said Clover. "This complicates things. Now we have a choice of ways."

They walked to the signpost and stared up. Rough letters were carved into two of the arms—the ones pointing to the sides. The arms pointing to the main Path were blank.

"What does it say?" asked Wilf. Sometimes he wished he had paid more attention at school. Then again, he had left when he was three. That was hardly enough time to find out where the bathroom was, let alone master the alphabet. He envied Clover's ability to read. She hadn't been to school either, but she was lucky. Her Pa had taught her to spell words. He said it would come in handy, and he was right.

"Cl—Clow—Clown Co—Co-leg. College, I mean. *Clown College*," read Clover, pointing to the left. "How strange. And that way is Yo—Young Ladies' Fi—Fishing—no, *finishing*. Finishing Aca—academy. *Young Ladies' Finishing Academy*." She pointed right.

"What's that?"

"A school for posh, rich girls."

"Where they fish?"

"No. Forget fishing. Where they paint and dance and drink tea and order the servants around."

"And then they're finished?"

"Yes. They get a certificate."

"A fish'd be more useful. How do you know all this?"

"Millie Higgins from the village was a maid in one of the big, fancy houses in town for a bit. She said the daughter went to a school like that. She went around putting on airs and boasting just because she'd got a better hat on."

"Who, the daughter?'

"No, Milly. You work in the shop. Don't you ever hear the gossip?"

"Not if I can help it."

"Ma says Milly never stopped talking about how well it paid, but everyone noticed she didn't go back. She's working at the Axes, now Tilly Adams has run off with the peddler man."

"Your Ma's working in the Axes?"

"No. *Milly*, silly."

"Oh. Really?" Wilf was getting bored with too much detail. He peered up at the signpost. "What's straight ahead?"

"It doesn't say."

"Now what do we do?" pondered Wilf. "Which way would Herby go, do you think? Straight on, or down one of the side roads?"

"We'll have to try all three," said Clover with a sigh. "It'll take a while, though."

"Not if we split up."

Clover thought about this. Was it a good idea? It would certainly save time. On the other hand . . .

She stared off into the too-green trees. She wished Mrs. Eckles were there to tell her what to do. She reached into her basket and took out the mirror. Her own face looked back at her. It looked anxious. She patted her hair, smoothed her brow, and hastily put the mirror away.

"It's too soon," said Wilf. "She won't have had time to get the Ball yet, don't you think?"

"I don't know. Time works differently here, remember?"

"Well, we can't hang about. Anyway, they don't sound *that* perilous, do they? Clowns and rich girls. What can they do?"

"We don't know, do we? Mrs. Eckles said that things aren't always what they seem. It might be some sort of trick."

"So we'll be on our guard. We'll just pop along, make inquiries, and then meet up back here. Unless you're too—" He stopped himself just in time. He had been going to say *too scared to go without me.*

"What? Too what?"

"Nothing."

"Were you about to say 'too scared to go without you'?"

"Certainly not. As if. No way." He wavered under Clover's gaze and added, "All right, then, yes, but I'm sorry. Stop glaring. You decide."

"All right," decided Clover. "We'll split up. It'll save time. Who'll do what?"

"I'll do Clown College," said Wilf, quick as a flash. "I've never seen a clown. They're funny, aren't they?"

"Supposed to be," said Clover doubtfully.

She thought about the painted cart that had passed by when she was little and Pa was still working. The others hadn't been born then. She remembered the lady in the dirty pink frock who stood on pointed toes. And the man in the red coat with the top hat. And the dancing bear, who she had felt sorry for because it looked sad.

But most of all, she remembered the clown. He had a white face and big red painted-on lips. He had seen her staring and poked his tongue out. It was the last time she had cried. She'd had bad dreams for weeks, then pulled herself together, grown up a bit, and got sensible.

"Well, I could do with a laugh," said Wilf. "It's all been a bit heavy, hasn't it? Herby and Old Barry and the bridge and that. And I don't like the sound of the young ladies."

"Scared of girls?" teased Clover.

"A bit," admitted Wilf. "I'm not good with posh people."

"You think I am?"

"At least you're a girl. I'm a boy; they'll probably attack me. Run my trousers up the flag pole. Laugh at my ears."

"More likely they'll ignore you. You'll be beneath their contempt."

"No point in me going then, is there? You'll have to."

"All right," said Clover. Privately, she was rather relieved. "But we ought to keep in touch in case there's trouble. *I'll* be all right, but what about you?"

"What, dealing with clowns?" said Wilf with a light little laugh. "I think I'll cope. But you're right, we should keep in touch. Can you whistle?"

"I've never tried. Can you?"

Wilf gave a rather cocky smile, stuck two fingers in his mouth and blew a shrill, piercing note that bounced around the treetops, echoing eerily. It was the sort of whistle you could hear for miles.

"Wow!" said Clover, surprised. "I didn't know you could do that."

"You never asked. It's easy. Try. Fingers like this, behind your teeth and blow."

Clover put her fingers behind her teeth and blew. To her surprise, after a couple of tries, her whistle was as strong and loud as Wilf's.

"You're a natural," said Wilf, approvingly. "We'll do a code. One short, cheerful blast every so often, say every fifty paces, to let the other know we're okay. A long, despairing one if there's trouble. Ready?"

"Ready."

"Right. Here we go, then. Good lu—no, actually, forget I said that. We make our own luck, right?"

"Right."

And with that, they parted.

CHAPTER TEN

Miss Fly Feels Guilty

"So, Fly," said Mesmeranza. "Have you posted the letter?"

Cold morning light poured through the windows of the turret room. A tray sat on the desk, containing the remains of a late breakfast.

"Yes," said Miss Fly, wiping her nose with a sodden hanky. "First thing this morning."

"You put in the snippet of rag?"

"Oh, yes. Of course. Most certainly."

Miss Fly stuffed the hanky back down in her cardigan pocket. In doing so, her fingers brushed against the letter. The letter she had copied, gotten Mesmeranza to sign, placed in an envelope together with a scrap of rag, sealed with wax, and affixed a stamp to.

The letter she hadn't posted.

"Good," said Mesmeranza. "That means it should arrive tomorrow. Very well, that's all for now. I'm going on the Ball. I wish to inspect the bait. Shut the door, I am not to be disturbed."

As soon as Miss Fly had scuttled from the room, Mesmeranza turned to the Crystal Ball that sat on the side table. She picked it up and waved a hand over the top.

"The Lodge," she commanded, crisply. "Show me."

The gray mist remained just that—gray mist.

"The *Huntsman's Lodge*," repeated Mesmeranza, louder. She gave the Ball an impatient shake.

A crackling, tinny, disembodied voice came from somewhere within. It said, "All dimensions are currently busy. Putting you on hold."

This was followed by an annoyingly scratchy little background tune that you couldn't quite hear.

Mesmeranza tutted and tapped her foot. After a

minute or two of this—dull gray mist, annoying tune, tutting and tapping—she lost patience and banged the Ball sharply on the arm of her chair.

"*Lodge!*" she snarled. "*Right now!*"

There was a bit more crackling and reluctantly—taking its time—the gray mist finally began to clear. The music faded away to nothing.

Slowly, a grainy picture formed. A timbered building set in a wood. There was a log pile outside, with what looked like a miniature axe set in a tree stump. But it was hard to make out. In fact, the picture as a whole was far from clear. It was fuzzy around the edges and flickering really badly, like an old black-and-white film.

"Zoom in," instructed Mesmeranza. "*Closer.* Go right inside, I wish to see the child."

The picture stubbornly remained the same. Mesmeranza tapped the Ball with a sharp talon.

The picture remained the same. Mesmeranza threw the Ball at the far wall. It fell, rolled back, and came to a stop at her feet.

There was no picture at all now. Not even mist.

Mesmeranza let out a little hiss of frustration. Typical. Another power failure. And at such a critical time, too. That was the trouble with the old Balls. You couldn't rely on them. Perhaps she should treat herself to a new one, out of the catalogue. One of those modern ones. And while she was at it, she would look for some new shoes. Yes, that's what she would do. New Plan, new Ball, new shoes. Purple, perhaps, to go with her dark mood.

"Fly!" she shrieked. "Come back here! What have you done with the catalogue?"

There was no reply. Miss Fly was long gone.

Humperdump Chunk sat spilling over his chair in the guard room, wishing he hadn't eaten the last doughnut and hoping that Jimbo Squint would hurry up and return with some more. Jimbo was up in the kitchens on a break and was, as usual, taking his time. Humperdump was getting bored down in the dungeons, alone with his thoughts. His thoughts were really depressing these days, since the love of his life had made her feelings clear. The only thing that cheered him up was food. Perhaps he would go up and have a second breakfast. On the other hand, that meant moving.

His ears pricked up at the sound of footsteps coming down the stone steps. Mind you, it didn't sound like Jimbo. Jimbo wore boots. These footsteps were lighter. They sort of—slapped. Flopped.

There came the sound of a stifled sneeze. Could it be? Surely not!

"Ah," said a voice from the doorway. "Chunk. I want a word with you."

It was! His lost beloved, there in the flesh! But why? Had she come to taunt him?

Humperdump stared warily at Miss Fly, taking in everything he had once admired about her. The frizzy, flyaway hair. The red, flaring nostrils. The hairy cardigan. The wide-fitting shoes. The faint odor of cat. Everything. How should he react? He couldn't take any more cruel rejection, but suppose she had changed her mind and realized that she had feelings for him after all? He decided to play it safe and gave a noncommittal grunt.

"Nng?"

"I'm hoping you can be of help," Miss Fly went on.

"Nng?" grunted Humperdump again. He didn't know where this was going.

"Look," continued Miss Fly, flushing a bit. "Look, I know this is a little awkward. With . . . er . . . our little . . . what happened a while back. The little . . . *misunderstanding*."

There was a long pause. Humperdump licked his lips and mumbled something.

"I beg your pardon?" asked Miss Fly. "You spoke?"

"I wrote you notes!" burst out Humperdump. He couldn't help it. She had to know how he had suffered.

"Yes," agreed Miss Fly tightly.

"I wrote you a rhymin' pome. About flowers."

"Mmm." Miss Fly's cheeks were as red as her nose.

"I brung you a cat. I found it an' brung it to you."

"Not one of *mine*, though, was it?"

"I didn't know that, did I? Thort I was doin' the right thing. You stomped on my foot and called me names. Got me in trouble with *Her*."

"Yes, well, that's all in the past. I'm not here to talk about that."

"What *are* you 'ere for then?"

"Information," said Miss Fly. "Tell me, how does a bag of gold sound?"

Humperdump thought. It sounded pretty good to him. But he didn't want to seem too easy.

"How big?" he asked cunningly.

"Very big. A great big golden sack. With 'GOLD' written on the side in big gold letters. Would you like a moment to think about it?"

"No, no, that's all right," said Humperdump quickly. "What d'you want to know?"

"Directions," said Miss Fly. "I've heard you some- times go out drinking with her ladyship's head hunts- man, yes?"

"What, Hybrow? Oh yer. He's a big mate o' mine, old Hybrow. I sees 'im an' his brothers Blud an' Gory once in a while. We meets up, 'as a laugh, a few jars."

This was actually an exaggeration. Hybrow and his brothers were more Jimbo's friends than his. Humper- dump just trailed along. But he didn't want Miss Fly to think he was sad and friendless.

"So you've visited the Hunting Lodge?"

"Once or twice. Mostly, they comes 'ere. For mum's cookin'."

"Their mother doesn't cook?"

"They don't live with their mum," explained Hump- erdump.

"They don't?" asked Miss Fly sharply. "Are you sure about that? No kindly old lady hovering around who might, for example, give soapy baths to small boys with nits?"

"Eh? Er . . . no. Just the lads."

"I see," said Miss Fly thoughtfully, adding, "and where *is* the Lodge, exactly?"

"It's a bit of a hike," Humperdump told her. "Out the castle, down the mountain. Time it right, and you can hitch a lift to the village on the milk cart. Then you takes the Number Three coach over the next mountain. Get orf at the next village. Then you changes onto the Number Eight, that'll take you to over the next pass, where you can pick up the husky sledge—"

"And how long will all this take?" interrupted Miss Fly.

"Best part of a day. Depends if there's an avalanche. Why d'you wanna know?"

"That's a private matter," said Miss Fly firmly, adding, "and I'd be grateful if you'd forget about our little chat."

"That's it?"

"That's it. Good day."

And Miss Fly turned and scuttled away.

"What about the bag o' gold?" shouted Humperdump. There was no reply.

* * ★ * *

Miss Fly hurried up the winding stairs to her apartment. It had gone better than she had hoped. It had been embarrassing, of course, but she had achieved what she had set out to do.

Miss Fly had thought long and hard about her boss's latest scheme. There were many things about it that bothered her. In fact, she had hardly slept at all the previous night. Not because Tabitha and Oliver had both peed on her pillow, which happened most nights, but because she didn't want to be party to such a wicked plan.

Miss Fly didn't know much about children. She preferred cats. But she didn't agree with child cruelty. Snatching away an innocent toddler from his family seemed to her to be going one step too far. Besides, the huntsman had obviously lied about his mother. What else might he be keeping secret?

She felt she should take steps. At least satisfy herself that the child was being well cared for. Fed and watered and still in one piece. If he seemed safe and well, that was different. But if not, she should really take a stand. Somebody had to take some responsibility.

Of course, her ladyship wouldn't welcome any interference. But then again, she didn't have to know, did she?

Miss Fly had some half-baked idea of popping along to the Lodge, sizing up the situation, and, if necessary, whisking the child away and returning him in secret to his mother. Hopefully, it wouldn't come to that. But her conscience insisted that she take some action.

CHAPTER ELEVEN

Clown College

The road leading to Clown College was different from the main Path. It wasn't straight. It twisted and turned all over the place. Sometimes, it became so narrow that the trees met overhead, forming a tunnel.

After striding out for fifty paces, Wilf stopped in his tracks, put his fingers in his mouth, and whistled. To his relief, Clover's answering whistle came back. So far, so good.

He walked on. He had hardly gone another ten paces before he heard—music? Yes, music! Loud, jolly music coming from somewhere up ahead.

He rounded a bend—and nearly walked headfirst into a gate!

It was a tall, wooden gate, painted in clashing colors. There was a big bunch of balloons tied to the gatepost. They bobbed around wildly, straining at their strings, although there was no wind.

Wilf stared up at the gate. It had no handle, no knob, no bell pull. But that didn't put him off. He was used to awkward gates. Mrs. Eckles had one.

"Open up," said Wilf briskly. He prepared himself for the usual argument.

The gate said nothing. It was obviously not a magic one, then.

It was then that he noticed the hole. A small, circular knothole, conveniently set at eye level. Wilf stepped up to the hole and peered in. He jumped back with a yell as a stubby rubber finger shot out and poked him in the eye!

"Arrgh!" wailed Wilf, staggering around, clutching at his eye. When he finally looked up, blinking through tears, the finger had retreated back into the hole and the gate stood invitingly open. The music blared out even louder.

Beyond lay a too-green field. In the middle of the field stood a huge circus tent. A number of smaller, brightly colored tents were dotted around—but it was the large one that drew the eye.

If the gate was odd, the big tent was off the scale. It was a riot of multicolored stars, stripes, spots, whirls, and swirls, and a big flag flew proudly from the center pole—although, of course, there was no breeze. The picture on the flag showed a big pair of flapping red lips. They looked like they were laughing.

The blaring music came from inside. Up close you could hear that it was distorted. There was a sort of unpleasant crackle in it.

Suddenly, the music stopped, as though a finger had flipped a switch. Then—from inside the tent—a voice spoke. Just two words.

"FUN TIME."

Innocent words. Playful words. So why did they send a chill up the spine? Probably because of the voice that spoke them. There was nothing jolly about that voice. It reminded Wilf of spiders and attics.

There came a low buzzing noise from the smaller,

outlying tents. Wilf watched, still tenderly fingering his watering eye, as a dozen flaps burst open . . .

And out poured clowns! Clowns of all shapes and sizes. Tall ones, short ones, fat ones, thin ones. Clowns in wigs, checkered jackets, and baggy trousers. Clowns with silly hats, red noses, and ridiculously long shoes. The one thing they had in common was that they all had big, smiley, painted red mouths.

Some turned somersaults and cartwheels. A couple walked on their hands! One of them wobbled around on stilts. Some just ran around in a silly way—skipping and waving their arms about and pretending to fall over. Others were carrying pies, still steaming and piled on top of each other. Several had big brushes and buckets filled with a variety of substances—red paint, pink slime, and something yellow that looked like custard.

A small clown dressed as a nanny raced around with a wheelbarrow containing a big clown in a pink baby bonnet, who was waving a rattle dementedly. Two clowns were taking turns whacking each other with rubber mallets. There was a one-man-band clown, simultane-ously playing a drum, a trumpet, a triangle, and a pair of clashing cymbals. The noise he made was dreadful and way out of time with the music that had started up again from inside the tent, even louder than before.

Wilf stepped between the open gates, to get a better view.

"Hello," said a voice.

Standing to one side, back against the hedge, hidden from the rest of the field behind a small tree, was another clown.

He was quite small, and possibly quite thin, although it was hard to tell his shape because he was dressed to look fat. He wore a pair of baggy checkered trousers in a hideous shade of orange. They were held up with stupidly short suspenders, so that the waistline was up around his armpits. His puffy blouse-type shirt—also orange—had a high collar. Around his neck was a large bow tie in contrasting bright green. His polished shoes sported matching green bows. On his head was a green-and-orange checkered hat, like an upside-down flowerpot. His cheeks had red circles dotted on them, and his lips were painted in the traditional red smile. But what you noticed most about him were his huge, horn-rimmed spectacles. The lenses were so thick, they looked like they had been cut from the bottoms of jam jars.

For some reason, he appeared to be quite wet. There were drops running down the spectacles and splashes down his front.

Wilf edged sideways into the shadow of the tree.

"Hello," said Wilf, speaking quite loudly because of the music. "Um, what's going on here?"

"Fun time. Ten minutes, then back to lessons."

"That's *fun*?"

Wilf stared in disbelief. A clown in a stripy sweater had found a quiet space by the hedge and was miming trying to escape from an invisible box. A silly, running-around clown in purple pants came racing up and mowed him down, invisible box and all. Enraged, stripy sweater picked himself up, took off after purple pants, and aimed a kick at his backside. You could hear it connect. It wasn't mime.

"That's how we do it here," said the clown solemnly. "That's how we play." He took off his spectacles, wiped them on his pants, then settled them again on his nose. His hugely magnified eyes wobbled up at Wilf. "Are you a new boy?"

"Nope," said Wilf quickly. "I'm just here to make inquiries. I'm looking for a little kid. He's called Herby. You haven't seen him, I suppose?"

"No. I've been in class all morning. Until I got thrown out."

"Who's in charge here?" inquired Wilf.

"That'd be Dr. Odd. He's the principal. Is that a joke stick?"

"What?"

"Your stick. Is it made of rubber?"

"No. It's just a stick. Made from—a stick."

"Well, I like it."

"Er, thanks. So, which one's Odd? Well, they all are, but you know." Wilf glanced sideways, hoping that the clown would laugh at his little joke. He didn't. He just said, "Inside the tent."

Wilf thought about Mrs. Eckles's words of advice. *Don't go inside anywhere. Like buildings or caves.* Did that include tents?

"Well, I only need a quick word. Perhaps he could step out? It'd only take a minute."

"He doesn't come out at Fun Time. Just at night. He walks about in the dark cracking his knuckles and chuckling. That's his sort of fun."

"What about you?" said Wilf. "Why aren't you—having fun?"

"Not allowed. All Fun Times forbidden until I get my tie angles right." The clown pointed to the green bow tie around his neck. "Professor Edmund Hilarity said I have to stay out here and practice squirting."

"Squirting? What, your *tie* squirts?"

"Yes. There's a nozzle in the middle with a bulb attached. The bulb's in my pocket. There's a connecting tube."

"Show me," said Wilf.

"I'd better not. I haven't got the knack. I'm still on Basic Squirting. Everyone else has moved on to Water Cannon. It spins, too, you see. The tie. There's another bulb for air that makes it revolve. I get confused by which one to press. So I panic and press both. Then it revolves and sprays water at the same time."

"Tricky," said Wilf sympathetically. "Look, I ought to be—"

"Sometimes the bulb comes loose from the tube and all the water comes out and soaks the front of my trousers."

"Embarrassing," said Wilf. "Look, interesting as this is—"

"The whole point is to get someone smack in the eye. It's supposed to be a surprise. It doesn't work if they see you fiddling about with tubes and bulbs. I'll try if you really want me to, but I'm almost out of water."

"No, don't bother. I'm in enough pain already. See?" Wilf pointed to his eye, which was still smarting. "What kind of a way is that to welcome visitors?"

"At least you didn't get the bucket of jelly falling on you. Or the boxing glove." The clown gave a sigh and added, "What's your name?"

"Wilf. What's yours?"

"My real name's Philip Tidden. But my clown name's Toodly Pip. Toodly Pip the clown."

"Which do you like to be known by?"

"Philip Tidden."

"Good choice," said Wilf. "Toodly Pip's a bit annoying."

"I know. But I had to think of something quickly. When I first arrived, they all ran around, pointing and shouting, '*Whatever it is, 'tidden the clown!*'"

Wilf choked back a snigger. He thought it was quite funny, but Philip Tidden obviously didn't. Or didden.

"We all have to come up with our own names," Philip Tidden went on. "If it's too much like someone else's, you get accused of copying, and Dr. Odd rubs your hair with balloons in assembly. Everybody laughs."

"And that's clown punishment, is it?"

"Yes. It hurts, actually. But it's not as bad as Pie-ing."

"Let me guess. He throws pies at you?"

"Everybody does. You get spun around on a big wheel and the whole college takes turns. They get points for doing it in a funny way. You wouldn't want a Pie-ing."

"No, I certainly wouldn't," agreed Wilf. Being a clown didn't sound like fun at all. He asked, "What do you get Pied for?"

"Failing to see the funny side," said Philip Tidden, glumly. " 'Laughter Is All.' That's the college motto. The trouble is, I'm not really very funny."

"Well, at least you've got a good pair of comedy glasses there," said Wilf, to cheer him up. "They're hilarious."

"They're not comedy glasses, they're mine. I use them to see."

"Oh.

"So," said Wilf hastily. "Everyone's got a silly name, you say?"

"Yes. See him?" Philip Tidden pointed. He indicated a clown in a ginger wig, who had the one-man-band clown by the throat and was rhythmically bashing his head on his own drum.

"What, the maniac in the wig?"

"That's Cheeky Charlie Chuckles. He's horrible, especially to new boys. He filled my shoes with jam. Everyone laughed and he got a sticker. Can I hold your stick? Just for a moment?"

Wilf was about to hand it over, then hesitated.

"Hey, wait a minute," he said, grinning. "This is a trick, right? You're a clown. You're planning to bash me with it, aren't you? In a funny sort of way."

"No. I just want to hold it."

"Well, just for a minute, then," said Wilf. He handed over the stick. Philip Tidden took it, examined it thoroughly through his bottle-bottom glasses, waved it around a bit, then handed it back again.

"Thanks," he said politely. "It's very nice. Stick-y."

"How did you get here?" asked Wilf, curious. Philip Tidden didn't seem clown material. "Did you come along the Perilous Path?"

"No," said Philip Tidden. "My father brought me. I won a scholarship. I wrote a ten-page essay about why I want to be a clown. I got the top grade."

"You did?"

"Yes. I'm good at essays. It's the comedy I have trouble with."

"Why go to Clown College, then?"

"Father was anxious for me to give it a try. He and Mother are depending on me. They're rather serious. There's supposed to be a clown in every family. They think I'll liven up mealtimes."

"Can't you write and tell them you're not cut out for it?"

"All the pens around here explode. And the mailbox has a hand that comes out and pinches your nose. Besides, I don't want to disappoint them. What's the Perilous Path?"

"Eh?"

"You mentioned a Perilous Path. What's that?"

"You don't want to know. It's complicated. I don't have time to—"

"Uh-oh. Cheeky Charlie Chuckles is looking this way," said Philip Tidden suddenly. "He's spotted you. He'll tell Dr. Odd."

The ginger-wigged clown was indeed staring. Not chuckling, though. He let go of the dazed one-man band, who slumped to the grass. Then he began to walk in an exaggerated, crab-wise fashion toward the big tent. He stood with his back to the flap and hissed something sideways out of his grinning mouth.

The music stopped.

Instantly, all activity ceased. The clowns just froze where they were, even in the middle of whacking each other. There was a long, expectant silence. Then, slowly, they turned their heads as one and stared. First at Wilf. Then—again moving as one—at the tent. Then back to Wilf again. Then the tent. Only their heads moved. It was very unnerving.

Wilf tightened his grip on his stick.

The flap of the tent peeled away to one side, and inside . . .

Inside, there was darkness. Sheer, total blackness. And then the dry, creepy voice spoke once again.

"IT APPEARS WE HAVE A NEW BOY. WHAT FUN. COME IN, LAD."

The echoes died away. The clowns' faces turned again toward Wilf.

"Don't," said Philip Tidden, quietly, out of the corner of his mouth.

"I won't," agreed Wilf. He raised his voice. "Actually, I'm fine over here. I'm not stopping. Just here to make inquiries."

There was another long silence. Nobody moved.

"INQUIRIES?" repeated the voice, after an uncomfortable amount of time.

"I'm looking for a little lost kid. His name's Herby. Has he come this way?"

"IS THIS A JOKE?"

"What? No. Of course it's not a joke."

"BUT YOU DO HAVE A JOKE?"

"Well, no. Not that I can think of right now."

"THIS IS CLOWN COLLEGE."

"Well, yes, I—"

"WE DON'T DO TRAGEDY HERE."

"No, I realize that, but—"

"WE CARE NOTHING FOR LOST CHILDREN."

"Now, just a minute . . ."

"EVERYTHING IS AMUSING. LAUGHTER IS ALL."

"No, it isn't!" yelled Wilf, angry now. "Not always, it isn't! Some things are *serious*!"

There came a horrified gasp from the assembled clowns. It was as though he had said something really shocking.

"*YOU HAVE SPOKEN THE FORBIDDEN WORD!*" The voice from the tent boomed around the silent field. "*MAKE YOUR CHOICE, BOY. JOIN US AND LEARN TO LAUGH. OR, ALTERNATIVELY, PREPARE FOR A PUBLIC PIE-ING!*"

A moan went up from the watching clowns. It sounded . . . expectant. Gleeful. It wasn't a pleasant sound.

Wilf thought about this. Enter the tent or be thrown to the clowns. Two choices.

No, three. Three choices.

Run!

CHAPTER TWELVE

Finishing Academy

Clover's road started out by being twisty and turny, just like Wilf's. But then it began to change. It became straighter and wider. The tangled trees gave way to a tall, clipped, too-green hedge that towered up on either side. The rough ground smoothed out and eventually she was walking on clean white gravel.

From somewhere far behind came a faint whistle. Wilf was checking in. Clover turned, put her fingers in her mouth and whistled a shrill reply.

When she turned back again, a short way up ahead was a high stone archway. Set in a wall to one side was a brass plaque bearing the inscription:

YOUNG LADIES' FINISHING ACADEMY
NO VISITORS WITHOUT APPOINTMENT
HEAD TEACHER: MISS TOYTT-HOITY

Beyond the arch lay a sweeping driveway bordered by velvety green lawns and neat flowerbeds. In the distance, tiny figures moved about with wheelbarrows and rakes. Gardeners, presumably. The driveway led to a grand house—a mass of spires, turrets, and elegant windows.

Clover hesitated. Mrs. Eckles had said not to go in anywhere. Did archways count? Under wasn't the same as in, was it?

It was then that she heard the sound of tinkling laughter. It came from behind the hedge to one side. She noticed a small barred gate set in the shrubbery.

She stepped up to the gate and peered through. A short distance away, a group of girls were having a tea party on the lawn. It was a charming scene. There were tables set with teapots, sugar bowls, cups and saucers and plates piled high with dainty sandwiches and fancy cakes. Some of the girls were perched on chairs, sipping tea. Others wandered around arm in arm, nibbling on cakes.

They were dressed in frilly frocks with matching satin sashes. Pale pastel colors seemed to be the order of the day. Powder blue, pale lemon, pale green, lavender, pink. All of them wore little white buttoned shoes. Several carried parasols, and one or two wore frilly bonnets.

Clover stared enviously. How she would love to join them. Just put her feet up and relax with a cup of tea and a little iced cake for ten minutes. Her stomach was growling, and her old boots were beginning to hurt her feet from all the walking.

"Excuse me?" she called.

But nobody heard her. Something else had caught their attention. Another group of frilly-frocked girls were approaching across the lawn, led by a cross-looking girl in pink.

"Who said you could have tea here, Anthea Spittlepick?" demanded the new pink girl, drawing up short. She had curly yellow hair and an upturned nose.

"What's it to you, Hortensia Howdairu?" snapped a girl from the first group. She had brown ringlets and was also wearing pink.

"Well, it just so happens that Miss Toytt-Hoity said we could practice our play here. So you can all move."

"Ooh!" squealed Anthea Spittlepick. "Such lies! I asked Miss Toytt-Hoity, and she said we could, so there!"

They stood nose to nose. Behind them, their supporters closed ranks.

"Liar? *Me*?" Hortensia Howdairu gave a short, sharp laugh. "Ha! *I* know you copied a poem from a book and said you made it up, and I'm *telling*. And why are you wearing pink? *I* always wear pink. I chose it first. You're just copying me, isn't she, Binkle?"

"Yes," agreed one of her acolytes, dressed in blue. "Hortensia always wears pink. She chose it first. You're just copying her, Anthea!"

"I am not! I can wear pink if I like!" snapped Anthea. "You're not the boss, Hortensia. Is she, Bubbles?"

"No," agreed a plump girl in green. "Leave Anthea alone, Hortensia, she can wear what she likes."

"Oh, *can* she? *Can* she?" sneered Hortensia. "Anyway, you can't talk, Bubbles Tiara, you're so fat you're *bursting* out of that dress, and anyway, *my* father says *your* father hasn't got a penny to his name. He can't even afford to pay for your harp lessons. You'll be thrown out of this school and nobody will miss you, and you won't get finished, so you won't marry royalty, but you wouldn't anyway because you're so ugly. *And* your petticoat's showing."

Bubbles Tiara burst into hysterical sobs. Members of her team crowded around to comfort her, patting and stroking and casting grim looks over their shoulders at Hortensia Howdairu and her frilly gang, who looked smug and very pleased with themselves.

Clover could hardly believe her ears. All those luxuries—pretty clothes and nice things to eat—and they were so hateful and mean. It seemed that money and a fancy education weren't all they were cracked up to be.

"You shouldn't talk, Hortensia Howdairu!" spat Anthea. "*My* mother went to lunch with *your* mother and she said you don't even have a second butler. So you won't marry royalty either. And I'm telling Miss Toytt-Hoity you made Bubbles cry. Take no notice, Bubbles, she's not worth it."

"Boo-hoo!" wailed Bubbles Tiara damply. "Boo-hoooooo!"

"Excuse me?" said Clover again, louder this time.

This time, they heard. Everyone stopped and stared. Dozens of eyes bored into her. They didn't look friendly.

"Servants' entrance around the back," snapped Hortensia Howdairu.

"I'm not a servant," said Clover. "I'm making inquiries. I'm looking for my little brother. He's wearing a cut-down flour sack and a red hat. Has he come this way?"

"I really have no idea," snapped Hortensia Howdairu. "Get lost, why don't you?"

"Yes, just clear off," agreed Anthea Spittlepick. "Can't you see we're busy? We couldn't care less about your stupid brother and his awful clothes."

They pointedly turned their backs on Clover and faced up to each other again.

"Anyway, Anthea, pink has always been *my* color, and . . ."

"Anyway, Hortensia, I can wear what I like . . ."

"Ninnies," said Clover, loudly and clearly. She just couldn't help it. There was a short, shocked silence.

"What?" said Anthea Spittlepick. "*What* did she just say?"

"You heard," said Clover. "Horrid, snobby, simpering, unhelpful, brainless ninnies. That's you."

The young ladies were gaping at her like goldfish. It was as though their brains had jammed. Nobody knew what to do. They just stared. Clover stared right back. She knew she would win. She was good at staring.

"Oh, look!" Suddenly, a girl dressed in pale lemon spoke up. "There goes Petula Plodfoot, in those *awful* pants."

And the spell was broken. The Young Ladies simultaneously turned their backs on the rude outsider in the faded dress and turned with relief on one of their own.

"Look at her *hair*," said one in turquoise with a sniff. "What a *mess*!"

"She must be running away again," said Bubbles Tiara eagerly. She had stopped crying. "Let's tell Miss Toytt-Hoity!"

A girl was marching down the driveway. Unlike the others, she wasn't wearing a frilly frock. She was dressed in a shabby old jacket and battered riding boots. A riding hat was under one arm. Her other hand held a suitcase. She had untidy brown hair that clearly hadn't seen a comb for some time.

"*We* see you, Petula Plodfoot!" shouted Hortensia Howdairu. "We're telling Miss Toytt-Hoity!"

"Yes!" chimed in the others. Both gangs seemed

united on this one. "She'll send out the gardeners. *Then* you'll be in trouble!"

The girl ignored them and marched on, through a hail of threats, jeers, and unkind comments about her appearance.

Clover stepped away from the gate and waited. Seconds later, the girl came striding through the archway. She drew level with Clover, gave a nod, and said, quite cheerfully, "Morning! Fine day!" Then strode on.

"Um, excuse me?" said Clover. She ran to catch up with her. Behind, the jeering died away. Presumably they had all gone running to tell Miss Toytt-Hoity.

"Yes?" The girl showed no signs of stopping. "Can I help?"

"I've lost my brother," said Clover. "Have you seen him? Herby's his name. Three years old, wearing a brown sack."

"No," said the girl. "'Fraid not, sorry. I suppose you asked that group?"

"Yes. They told me to leave."

"Typical. Give me horses any day. Better manners, absolutely. I always ignore 'em."

"So I saw. Um, are you really running away?"

"Yup. I do it two or three times a week."

"In broad daylight?"

"Makes no difference. They always catch me and bring me back."

"So why do it?"

"Well, it's nice to get away from that lot for a bit. Bit of an outing, bit of fresh air. Until the gardeners show up."

"Gardeners?"

"That's what Hoity Toit calls them. Hired thugs, more like."

"What's she like?" asked Clover, curious. "Miss Toytt-Hoity?"

"Think of a smiley snake in half glasses. She wasn't smiling when I made a bonfire of the ghastly frock she tried to make me wear, mind. Pale lavender. Can you imagine?"

"Did you get into trouble?"

"Oh, absolutely, but I don't care. I'm trying to get expelled, you see. Cause enough bother and she'll send me home. She's already sent three warning letters to Popsy. It's just a matter of time."

"Popsy?"

"My father. That's what I call him."

"Really? I call mine Pa. What does your father do?"

"Not much. He's a rich landowner. He gives absolutely loads to the poor, though."

"Pa's a poor woodcutter. I've never seen him give to the rich." They caught each other's eye and laughed. Clover added, "Actually, he doesn't do much either. He hurt his back lifting a pig, though we did tell him not to."

"Fathers," said the girl. "They're all the same. They never listen."

"You're right," agreed Clover. "If mine had listened to Ma and fixed the gate, we wouldn't have lost Herby."

"And if mine had listened to me, I'd be mucking out the stables instead of wasting time going to finishing school."

"You don't want to get finished, then?" panted Clover. It was quite hard to keep up.

"Absolutely not. Didn't even wanted to get *started*. Especially when I found out I couldn't bring Strawberry Shortcake."

"S . . . ?"

"Strawberry Shortcake, my pony. Shorty for short. He'll be missing me terribly by now. He's fourteen hands. Chestnut, with a white blaze and socks. Terribly intelligent, he can count up to three. Best in Show three years running. Do you ride?"

"No. Just walk."

"Well, you should, it's a lot quicker. I'm Petula Plodfoot. What's your name?"

"Clover. Clover Twig."

"What are you doing around here? Do you live nearby?"

"No. Not really. It's a bit hard to explain."

"Where are you off to now?"

"Back to the signpost. I'm meeting a friend there."

"Signpost?" Petula Plodfoot sounded puzzled. "There's no signpost around here."

"I think you'll find there is. Up ahead. On the Perilous Path."

"The what?"

"The Perilous Path. That's what I'm on. Well, right now we're together, so I suppose you're on it too. You should probably turn back, while there's time."

"I haven't a clue what you're talking about," said Petula, "but it sounds interesting. Are you on some sort of adventure?"

"I suppose you could say that. The Path turned up in the forest, you see, and Herby wandered off down it. Mrs. Eckles saw him. She's the Witch I clean for. It's a long story."

"Excellent! I love adventure stories," said Petula cheerfully. "And I've got all day. At least until the gardeners come. Why don't you tell me about it?"

CHAPTER THIRTEEN

Ball Trouble

"So you smashed it with a frying pan."

Thick green smoke drifted around the lamp-lit kitchen. Mrs. Eckles stood before her private cupboard, in deep conversation with an Imp. In her hand was the bag containing the mess of hopelessly mangled pieces that had once been the Ballmaster Multidimensional

Mark Six. Neville sat at her feet, gazing up at the Imp and licking his lips.

The Imp's name was Bernard. He was small and green from the tip of his bald head down to his horny bare feet. Beard, ears, nose, webbed hands, toenails, jerkin, pants—everything green. Over his shoulder was a green sack containing the magic bubble needed to fly the cottage. All flying cottages come with an Imp. Some are more obliging than others.

"Yes," said Mrs. Eckles. "I just told you. It was makin' a funny noise."

"I cannot *believe* you did that," snapped Bernard irritably.

The Summons had come right when he was in the middle of breakfast. He'd had to drop everything, grab the bubble sack, navigate through six dimensions at the speed of light, and materialize with a dramatic explosion in a magic portal while still chewing on a mouthful of bacon.

The arrival had been a shambles too. Mrs. Eckles had no respect for magic portals. To her, a cupboard was a cupboard. She kept all her private stuff in there, crammed in any old way, and, as usual, she hadn't bothered to clear him a decent space. Bernard was crammed on the middle shelf between a dusty jar and a bunch of scratchy herbs that kept catching on his pants. Even more annoying, he needn't have brought the magic bubble since Mrs. Eckles didn't want to fly anywhere.

"I thought it was gonna blow," said Mrs. Eckles.

"So you smashed it with a frying pan."

"Yes. I had to stop it wailin'."

"By smashing it with a frying pan."

"Yes! I had to think about Neville's whiskers."

"So you smashed it with a fr—"

"Yes! *Yes!*" cried Mrs. Eckles. "Stop *sayin'* that. The thing is, what do we do about it?"

"*We?* Oh, no." Bernard shook his head. "You're not involving me. Not my job. I'm a *Flying* Imp. You want a favor, you need a Good Deed Imp."

"I ain't got a Good Deed Imp," Mrs. Eckles pointed out. "I've only got you."

"My function is to fly the cottage. I don't fix vandalized magical equipment."

"But I dare say you know someone who does. You got contacts, ain't you?"

"I might have, and I might not. The rules state—"

"Ah, to heck with the rules!" roared Mrs. Eckles. "I got a situation here! I got three kids on the Perilous Path! Clover, Wilf, and Little Herby! They need help, and I gotta get through!"

"The Perilous Path?" Bernard's eyebrows shot up and down very quickly. Then he began shaking his head and giving knowing little whistles. "That's turned up again, has it? Oh, deary dear. You've got a problem there."

"I know! So do you know where I can get this bloomin' Ball fixed or don't you?"

"Well . . . possibly," admitted Bernard grudgingly. "There's an Elf I know fixes broken appliances."

"Take it to 'im. Tell 'im it's a good cause, I might get a discount. Say it's high priority, he's to drop everythin'. Here." Mrs. Eckles held out the jingling bag. "Go. Now."

"All right." Bernard sighed. "I'll see what I can do. But this is all very inconvenient. Put it in, then."

Mrs. Eckles made room on the shelf by swiping a few of the bottles onto the floor. It was the way she did things when Clover wasn't around. She placed the jingling bag next to Bernard, who said, "I want it on the record that you summoned me on false pretenses. And I'm claiming for overtime—"

Mrs. Eckles slammed the cupboard door.

★ ★ ★ ★ ★

Granny Dismal sat in her cottage, staring down at her backup Crystal Ball, which was an old Stargazer Three. It was nowhere near as fancy as the Ballmaster Multidimensional Mark Six. It didn't have any little levers or buttons and relied on old-fashioned hand movements, but it was built to last and it did the job. Despite her fury with Demelza Eckles taking off like that, Granny Dismal had put all thoughts of revenge to simmer on the back burner and concentrated on the job at hand—breaking the latest sensational news to her fellow Witches. Nobody could say she hadn't done her duty. She had contacted everyone. They all now knew that little Herbediah Twig had wandered off down the Perilous Path.

Outside, dawn was breaking and she hadn't even been to bed. She had been up all night talking to Mrs. Spool, Mrs. Frunk, Granny Gripefinger, Old Mother Flummox, Euphonia Mangle, Wanda the Wise Woman of Wibbleton, Nanny Nubbins, Goody Twinge, and Gammer Spindle. They had all expressed regret. They had sighed and tutted and promised to keep their eyes, ears, and noses to the ground. Although you would never believe it from the stories, most village Witches are protective of small children. None of them offered to go in after him, though, so not *that* protective.

That was everybody. Everybody that came to the potluck evenings, anyway. Of course, there was one Witch who never turned up. Mesmeranza Coldiron, Demelza Eckles's antisocial sister, who thought herself a cut above and put on airs. She had once returned her invitation to the Annual Halloween Fest ripped into small pieces, with a note saying, *I assume you are joking?*

Nevertheless, she should be put in the picture. Most likely she wouldn't give two figs, but Granny Dismal felt it her duty to get in touch. Demelza Eckles wouldn't like it, of course. There was no love lost between those two. But so what? She shouldn't have taken off with the Ballmaster like she did. It showed a complete lack of respect, and that's one thing that Witches demand.

Granny Dismal waved her hand over the Stargazer Three. Rather tiredly, it wheezed into life.

"Mesmeranza Coldiron," commanded Granny Dismal. "Full speed and power, it's urgent."

After a moment or two, the gray mist cleared, and she found herself staring into a face. A face with hard green eyes and a red-painted mouth. It didn't look too pleased to see Granny Dismal.

"Yes? What?"

"It's me," said Granny Dismal. "Ida Dismal. From Piffle."

"I can see that. So?"

"I'm the bearer of bad news," said Granny Dismal with chilly satisfaction. "There's something you should know."

"Well, get on with it, then. I need to make calls, and you're tying up the Ball."

"The Perilous Path's back. It's here in the forest. Saw it with my own eyes."

"Well, it's no concern of mine, is it? I don't live in the forest, so why should I care?"

"Just warning you," said Granny Dismal. "It's very active this time. It's already got its first victim. A local child. Herbediah Twig."

There was a short silence. Then, "*What?*"

"Little Herby Twig. He's gone wandering off down the Path."

"I don't *think* so."

"I *know* so," said Granny Dismal with smug triumph. "Your sister came to tell me about it. Came banging on the door. Got me out of bed."

"I think you'll find she was mistaken," said Mesmeranza coldly. "You should check your facts."

"I think you'll find I'm not," said Granny Dismal even more smugly. "She was very sure about it. I've been up all night spreading the wo—"

She broke off. Well, there was no point in talking to gray mist. Mesmeranza had cut the connection.

How rude. Try to do your duty and that's what you got.

Granny Dismal gave a sniff, rose, put another scarf on, and went off to make a fresh pot of herb tea.

* ★ ★ ★ ★

Back in Castle Coldiron, Mesmeranza sat bolt upright in her chair. She couldn't believe what she had just heard. Herbediah Twig not at the Lodge, having his nits attended to? Instead, he'd gone roaming down the Perilous Path? How was that possible? Had he escaped from the Lodge? Got all soapy and just slithered out of the bath and away? Or . . . surely not! Could the huntsman have lied through his teeth? Could it be that he *never had the child in the first place?*

The more she thought about it, the more it seemed that the latter was the likelier possibility. Come to think of it, he had been sweating a lot. All right, so he had secured the child's rag—but that didn't mean he had secured the actual *child*, did it?

Another thought occurred to her. What about Miss Fly? She had disapproved of the kidnapping plan all along. In fact, she had been a real Fly in the ointment, with her sniffs and negative comments. Could the two of them be in cahoots?

Mesmeranza rose, marched to the door, and wrenched it open.

"*Fly?*" she screamed. "Get in here this minute! I want a word with you!"

★ ★ ★ ★ ★

Miss Fly stood at the stable door with an empty cat basket, eyeing Booboo.

Booboo was munching hay and had his back turned. His wings were tightly folded.

"Are you sure about this, miss?" asked the groom, doubtfully.

"Quite sure," said Miss Fly. "He'll be putty in my hands. I have a natural way with animals. Well, I do with cats. A sort of mystic bond. Do you have a saucer of milk I can give him? So I can build up the trust?"

"He don't drink milk," explained the groom, adding, "and he don't take kindly to strangers ridin' 'im. If you don't believe me, ask the huntsman. Gave 'im the right runaround, didn't you, you swine?"

"I'm sure we'll get on just fine. Won't we, Booboo?" Miss Fly set down the basket and slapped forward to pat the twitching black rump.

As she approached, Booboo detected a musty odor. It was the unmistakable smell of cat. Well, Miss Fly lived with forty of them. It was hardly surprising.

Booboo didn't like cats. He had a real thing about them. He had a thing about a lot of things, but cats really spooked him. He tossed his head and swished his tail.

"You see?" Miss Fly stroked Booboo's rump. "See what I'm doing here? He's saying he likes it. He's wagging his head and swishing his tail; that tells me he senses I'm not a threat. Kindness, that's the key. You see the bond we're developing? You have to be very patient, and use a soothing tone . . ."

Booboo lashed out with his back hoof, narrowly missing her shin. Miss Fly reeled back, arms flailing.

"He ain't no cat," said the groom gloomily. "More like a . . . what shall I say? Fiend. That's it, a flyin' fiend."

"Nevertheless," said Miss Fly, straightening up, not quite so confident now. "Nevertheless, I have an urgent errand to do. I'm taking a cat to the vet. I'm sure we'll be great friends."

Booboo bared his yellow teeth in a leer and spat out a mouthful of soggy hay, which landed on her shoe.

"Takin' a cat to the vet, did you say?" The groom eyed the empty cat basket. "Well, it's a bit thin, I'll say that."

"Oh, did I say *taking*? I meant collecting. I'm *collecting* a cat from the vet. Look, I really am in rather a hurry. Saddle the horse, if you please."

"And 'er Ladyship's given consent?"

"Of course," lied Miss Fly.

"Needs to be in writin'."

"It does?" To give herself time to think about this, Miss Fly blew her nose long and hard. She balled up the hanky and stuffed it in her pocket. Once again, her fingers brushed against paper. A thought occurred to her. "Can you read, my good fellow?"

"No," admitted the groom. "But I needs it for me files."

Miss Fly produced the sealed envelope from her pocket and handed it over, imperiously.

"There. Written permission. Kindly do as I ask."

"Fair enough," said the groom, stuffing it down his shirt. "You want the usual saddle? Or the Saddle of Invisibility?"

"No, no," said Miss Fly hastily. "Just the usual one,

please." Riding a flying fiend would be tricky enough. She couldn't imagine sitting astride one you couldn't even *see*. Miss Fly had a fair head for heights as a result of dangling over canyons rescuing stuck kittens. But there were limits.

She fished into her pocket for another hanky. Her nose was beginning to stream and she didn't have her pills. It could be that she was allergic to horses as well as cats, but more likely it was nerves.

The truth was, Miss Fly was no horsewoman. Her experience was limited to childhood donkey rides at the beach. She had a feeling that the mystic bond she shared with animals would be severely stretched in Booboo's case. But she was committed now.

"And you're *sure* you can handle him?" fretted the groom. Booboo was now kicking a hole in a plank of his stall. Wood was splintering everywhere.

"Most definitely."

Miss Fly wasn't sure at all. But she needed to get to the Lodge, satisfy herself that the child was being well cared for, then return before Her Ladyship noticed she was gone. There wasn't time to take a million coaches over a million mountains. Speed was of the essence. Booboo was the only way.

Riding Booboo wasn't the only thing Miss Fly was

worried about. She dreaded what she might find on arrival. What if she found her suspicions confirmed? Supposing conditions at the Lodge were indeed intolerable? Who knew how rough huntsmen lived? What would they know about a little boy's needs? Miss Fly didn't know much about them herself, actually, but at least he wouldn't go short of milk and fish heads.

She really hadn't thought the whole thing through. Supposing she had to remove the child? Stuff him in the cat basket and somehow return him to the bosom of his family, although she wasn't even sure where they lived? All without Her Ladyship's knowledge?

Miss Fly's conscience didn't stretch that far. If her boss found out that she had interfered, she would be in deep trouble. She might even get fired! Then what? She had the cats to think about.

She watched the groom sidle up with the saddle. Booboo stopped kicking the plank in and tensed.

"Now then," said the groom. "None o' that, you swine."

He reached into his pocket and produced a sugar lump, which he tossed expertly. Booboo snatched it from the air and crunched it between large yellow teeth. His tail swished appreciatively. While he was thus engaged, the groom hastily began to saddle him up.

It was a kind of game. Booboo behaved as long as he had sugar. When the eyes rolled sideways and the jaws stopped working and the tail stopped swishing, the groom tossed him another lump.

"That's an awful lot of sugar," said Miss Fly disapprovingly.

"Only way to deal with him when he's in one of his moods. I'm sweetening him up for you. Twenty lumps or so should get you there. He'll need refilling for the return journey, though."

"Nonsense, I'm not giving him sugar."

"Suit yourself. But that's what he runs best on."

"He'll know which way to go, I assume?" asked Miss Fly. She wasn't sure how flying horses worked.

"Oh, yes. Just state the destination clearly in his ear and he'll work out the quickest route. It's called Flying Horse Sense. All you have to do is stay on."

"Right. Anything else I should know?"

"Well, he don't like the color purple," explained the groom, busily tightening straps and adjusting the harness. "And he shies at loud noises. Avoid scarecrows, he hates 'em. Watch out for bats and birds, he hates them too. When you dismount, he'll try to bite, so move away quickly, but don't go near his rear end or he'll kick you. Rein him in tight or he'll try and scrape you off on

treetops. Keep your mouth closed unless you want flies in your teeth. . . ."

Miss Fly nodded and made all the right noises, but she didn't really take it in. She knew she would forget every single tip when she was airborne. She would just hold on, close her eyes, and hope for the best. It had always worked with donkeys.

Finally, the groom came to an end.

". . . and he don't like mice, cats, dogs, orange peel, windmills, or paper bags. That's about it. Right, he's ready. Shall I give you a hand up, miss?"

So, then. This was the moment of truth.

Miss Fly stepped forward. Booboo started shaking his mane and pawing the ground, causing sparks to fly.

"Perhaps I will take the sugar," said Miss Fly.

CHAPTER FOURTEEN

Back on the Path

"Well, will you look at that!" cried Petula Plodfoot as she and Clover rounded a bend. "There *is* a signpost. How extraordinary."

"You see?" said Clover. "I told you."

"Who are those two up ahead?"

"That's Wilf, my friend, with the red hair. But I don't

know who the clown is." Clover raised her voice and shouted, "Any luck?"

"No," called Wilf. "You?"

"No. Who's this?" Clover walked up to the signpost, drew up short, and stared hard at Philip Tidden.

"Philip Tidden," said Wilf. "Phil, this is Clover, the friend I was telling you about."

"Hello," said Philip Tidden. Nervously, he plunged his hands into his pockets and his bow tie began to spin. A small dribble of water trickled out and dripped onto Clover's boot.

"He didn't like it at Clown College, and I don't blame him because they're funny all the time and it's creepy," went on Wilf. "We had to run like mad. He wants to come with us down the Perilous Path, don't you, Phil?"

"Yes, please," said Philip Tidden.

"And why not?" cut in Petula Plodfoot from behind. "More the merrier, eh?"

Wilf stared at her. "And you are . . . ?"

"Petula Plodfoot," Petula stuck out her hand. "Pleased to meet you. Absolutely."

"Petula's running away," explained Clover. "She hates it at the Young Ladies' Finishing Academy. They won't let her have Strawberry Shortcake. That's her pony."

Rather uncertainly, Wilf extended his hand and allowed it to be vigorously pumped up and down. Then he said, "Could I have a word, Clover? In private?"

"Funnily enough, I was going to ask you the same thing," said Clover. "Excuse me one moment, Petula."

"By all means," said Petula cheerfully. "Come on, Phil, tell me all about life as a clown. Sounds frightfully jolly."

"Well, no, actually, it's not," said Philip Tidden earnestly. "I've got this bow tie, you see, and there's bulbs in the pocket—one's for air and one's for water—and the problem is . . ."

Wilf and Clover moved out of earshot, leaving Petula Plodfoot and Philip Tidden to talk by themselves.

"What's he doing here?" snapped Clover.

"Coming with us."

"Who says? I don't remember agreeing to let anyone else trail along."

"What about her, then? Your horsy Plodfoot girl?"

"That's different. She's on the run. She just happens to be running in the same direction. Anyway, she's nice. It's good to talk to someone sensible for a change." "She doesn't sound sensible," snapped Wilf, a bit miffed. "Naming her horse after food . . . where's the sense in that?"

"At least she's not wearing orange trousers." Clover glared crossly at Philip Tidden, who was demonstrating how his bow tie revolved. Petula was nodding and looking interested.

"Well, what was I supposed to do? I couldn't leave him behind in Clown College. It's terrible there."

"It was awful at the Finishing Academy too. Those girls were *poisonous*. What's that got to do with anything?"

"I felt sorry for him. He only wants to help."

"What help can he be? Just look at him, he's a *joke*."

They both stared at Philip Tidden. He and Petula had wandered farther up the Path. Philip Tidden was stooped over, nose nearly touching the ground, inspecting something.

"He can't help the way he looks," argued Wilf. "He never wanted to be a clown. The tie's a terrible weight around his neck. He can't get the knack." Philip Tidden was showing whatever he had found to Petula. They both looked quite animated.

"Well, that's his problem. Besides, we've only got two sandwiches. And I don't like clowns."

"He's not like normal clowns. He's not a bit funny."

"I don't care if he's a laugh a minute. Tell him he's not coming."

"All right, then, if I must. He'll be upset, though. Phil! Come here a minute."

Philip Tidden came hurrying back, with Petula marching behind.

"I say," he said. "I think I've just—"

"Clover's got something to tell you," said Wilf lamely. He just couldn't do it.

"You can't come with us," said Clover bluntly. She flashed a sour glance at Wilf, who avoided eye contact.

"Why not?" Philip Tidden looked stricken.

"Because we haven't got enough food."

"I don't mind, I'm not hungry. I can be helpful. I can find twigs for a fire or something. Speaking of finding things, I th—"

"We're not *camping*. This isn't a Sunday picnic. We have to keep moving. We've got to find Herby. We're looking for clues, and we're in a hurry and I don't think you . . . well, your sight's not that great, is it? Unless those are comedy glasses?"

"They're not," muttered Wilf. "I've already asked."

"I see," said Philip Tidden. "Right. Clues." His magnified eyes swam sideways, to Petula, who nodded encouragingly. "You mean, like this?"

He held out his hand. In it was a yellow sweet wrapper.

There was a short, shocked silence.

"Where did you find that?" demanded Clover.

"Up the Path. Lying on the ground by a clump of grass."

"Eyes like a hawk," said Petula, clapping Philip Tidden on the back. "Amazing. Take him along, he's a real asset."

"It's my glasses," said Philip Tidden modestly. "They just make things bigger."

Wilf and Clover stared down at the wrapper, then at each other, then at Philip Tidden.

"Philip Tidden," said Clover. "I think I owe you an apology."

"So I can come?"

"Certainly. Wilf'll share his sandwich with you."

"All right," agreed Wilf, adding, "but I'd leave the tie behind, Phil. It just complicates things. You're not a clown now, you're a tracker. You don't see many trackers wearing bow ties."

"I can't," said Philip Tidden, a bit anxiously. "It's my only trick. I've got to get it right. My parents will be expecting a demonstration when I get home. Besides, it's attached to the shirt, and the shirt's attached to the trousers. Everything falls down if I take the tie off."

"Fine," said Clover hastily. "The tie comes too. But

I'll lend you my hanky and while we're walking you can wipe the big red lips off, if you don't mind. Come on, enough talk, let's go."

And she turned and began marching determinedly along the Path. Wilf and Philip Tidden gave each other a thumbs-up sign and set off in her wake. Petula picked up her suitcase and said, "Might as well join you, before the gardeners arrive."

"Gardeners?" said Wilf. "What gardeners?"

"It's a long story," said Clover. "Let's save it for later."

"I'm not sure she should come," said Wilf. He only had the one stick. How many more people was he supposed to protect?

"Don't worry about me," said Petula brightly. "I can look after myself. Anyway, people on adventures always meet interesting new friends and take them along."

"Who says you're interesting?" snapped Wilf. Everyone stared at him. Even Philip Tidden looked surprised. Wilf felt a bit guilty. It wasn't like him to be mean. The Path must be bringing out his worst side. He added, "Sorry. Let's go. After *you*, Petula."

The Path continued through the trees, just as before—except that it was no longer straight. It was bending around to the left. Clover took the lead, followed by Philip Tidden, then Petula. Wilf and his stick brought up the rear.

"This is amazing," said Petula, staring around interestedly as they hurried along. "I've certainly never been this way before. Absolutely not. It's really sinister, isn't it? Sort of a funny light . . ."

She broke off and bumped into Philip Tidden, who had stopped. The reason he had stopped was that Clover had come to a sudden halt and was holding up her hand.

"Listen!" she hissed. "Hear that?"

"What?" said Wilf. "I can't hear a thing."

"Me neither," agreed Petula.

"Or me," said Philip Tidden.

"*Listen*, why don't you? Somebody's chopping!"

Clover could hear the sound quite clearly. From somewhere up ahead came the distinct sound of an ax hacking into wood. There a pause between each strike, followed by an echo that bounced eerily around the treetops.

Chop! (*chop . . . chop . . . chop . . .*)
Chop! (*chop . . . chop . . . chop . . .*)
Chop! (*chop . . . chop . . . chop . . .*)

"Stay close," hissed Clover. "And be prepared to run."

Heart in mouth, she crept forward . . . and rounded the bend.

Up ahead was a tall figure. It stood to one side of the trail at the base of a tall tree. It had its back to them. It was staring upward and there was a long-handled ax in its gloved hand.

Clover gave a gasp. She knew that old gray jacket with the elbow patches! She knew those faded old trousers and those battered leather gloves and that ancient slouch hat! It couldn't be, could it? Could it really be him? But of course it was.

"*Pa!*" she screamed, starting forward. "*Oh Pa, it's me!*"

"Clover!" shouted Wilf. "Clover, don't . . ."

But he was too late. Clover was already racing down the Path, arms spread wide, braids flying, awash with relief and happiness.

The figure turned at her shout. Clover was running so fast, she couldn't stop. She had almost reached it before she suddenly registered that there was something terribly wrong. The shape was right, the clothes were right, the slouch hat was right . . .

But the face was wrong! The face was furry. It had a long gray snout. It had small yellow eyes and a grinning mouth lined with wickedly sharp teeth, from which

lolled a long, curling tongue. And from out of that mouth came a single, rasped word.

"Timmmmberrrrrrrrr!"

There was a terrible, sighing, creaking noise, and the crunching of high branches . . .

And with a groaning crash, the tree fell!

CHAPTER FIFTEEN

Two in Trouble

The Hunting Lodge sat in a large clearing. It was a big, timbered building with a veranda. The windows were small, dark, and dirty. A huge pair of antlers was mounted over the door. There was a log pile to one side, with a rusty ax jammed into a stump.

All was quiet, apart from the occasional cheep from a bird. And then . . .

Booboo landed! There was the sound of branches snapping and wild flapping followed by a mighty thump . . . and there he was, swishing his tail, rolling his eyes, snorting, and champing at the bit, quite spoiling the peaceful scene.

Clinging to his broad back was Miss Fly. Her frizzy

hair stood on end, like stuffing exploding from a sofa. Her eyes were tightly closed, but her mouth was open in the frozen aftermath of a scream. Amazingly, though, she still gripped the cat basket with a white-knuckled hand. The other hand held the reins, like that of a drowning person clinging to a lifeline.

It had clearly been no donkey ride.

Slowly, Miss Fly opened her eyes. Stiffly, she dismounted. Booboo slyly waited until she had one foot on the ground and one still in the stirrup, then veered sideways. Miss Fly desperately tried to hop with him.

"Now, now!" wailed Miss Fly. "Stand still! Behave, you naughty thing!"

The foot in the stirrup came free and she ducked and scuttled away, just as his head snapped around and his teeth flashed, missing her by a centimeter.

"Wait there!" instructed Miss Fly. "And behave yourself, or it's no sugar for you!"

Patting her hair, spitting out the odd fly and plucking leaves from her cardigan, Miss Fly stood staring at the Lodge.

It looked . . . deserted. There was no movement behind the windows. No sounds from within. No child-like laughter or boisterous drinking songs.

Miss Fly took a deep breath. Cat basket in hand, she

mounted the steps leading to the veranda and boldly approached the front door. It had a chain across it, secured with a large padlock.

There was a note too. A small scrap of paper, held in place with a rusty nail. Scrawled on the paper, in big, badly formed letters, was a single word:

CLOSD

As she stood inspecting it, there came the sudden, unmistakable sound of wheels coming from somewhere around the back. Miss Fly turned and scuttled back down the steps. She hurried to the side of the Lodge and was just in time to see a heavily loaded cart making off into the trees, pulled by a straining cart horse. She only caught a brief glimpse of the driver's back, but that was enough.

It was Hybrow Hunter!

The cart was piled high with furniture, including a large wardrobe, a grandfather clock, a bed, a wooden table, three high-backed chairs, and a number of antlers. Sitting on top of the pile were two big, hairy men dressed in green. Hybrow's brothers, Blud and Gory, presumably. They were laughing uproariously and passing a bottle between them.

"Stop!" shouted Miss Fly. "Stop right there! I'd like a word with you!"

But she was too late. The cart vanished in the trees, and the sound of its rumbling passage slowly faded away.

So. The huntsmen were fleeing the Lodge, taking their furniture with them. But where was the child? There had been no sign of him on the cart. Surely they wouldn't have left him behind?

Miss Fly made her way back onto the veranda and once again examined the door. Short of using a battering ram, there was no way she could get in.

"Hello?" she called. "Herbediah Twig? Are you in there?"

She applied her ear to the door. Total silence.

Miss Fly walked along the veranda to the nearest window. She stepped up close, rubbed the filthy pane with her cardigan sleeve, and was just about to apply her eye, when something stopped her. Something that made her stagger back with a startled little scream.

A face had appeared in the window. Not behind it. In the *actual glass*. It was a familiar face. A face that, right now, looked far from happy.

"Fly," hissed Mesmeranza. The glass rattled furiously in its frame. "I am on the Ball. What in the name of chronic stupidity do you think you're playing at? Get. Back. Here. *Right now!*"

Miss Fly nearly died.

* ★ ★ ★ ★ *

Back in the cottage kitchen, Mrs. Eckles was having less success than her sister at making contact on a Crystal Ball.

The problem wasn't the Ballmaster Multidimensional Mark Six, though. Mrs. Eckles's name obviously counted in Elf circles. One mention of Demelza Eckles and as quick as a flash it had been rebuilt, retuned, polished nicely, and sent back with Bernard in under ten minutes. What's more, she had even gotten a complementary pen, a handy bottle opener, some flowery stationery, and a year's free subscription to *Elf News*. Elves are wiser than Imps and like to keep on the right side of Witches.

No, the problem lay with Mrs. Eckles, who couldn't understand the instruction manual. She sat at the kitchen table frowning and flipping over pages while Bernard hovered in the cupboard, getting more irritable by the minute.

"Is this going to take much longer?" asked Bernard. "Because I've got my cousin coming over with his vacation pictures. We're having a soufflé."

"Oh, *riiiight*," jeered Mrs. Eckles. "Like that's

important. You'll go when I say you can. I need a bit of 'elp 'ere. There's all these diagrams and squiggles. Can't make head nor tail of 'em. *You* try."

"Give it here, then. I don't have elastic arms. You know I can't leave the portal."

This was true. The private cupboard contained a magical force field. Some weird rule dictated that Bernard had to stay within its confines or risk some kind of nasty Imp implosion. Apparently, it had happened to an uncle. It hadn't been fatal, just messy.

Mrs. Eckles walked to the cupboard and slammed the manual down at Bernard's feet, raising dust and causing his green beard to blow about.

"Go on. See if you can make sense of it."

"Shrink it down, then. I prefer to hold my reading matter rather than stand on it."

"Good grief! Anything else, your lordship? All right, all right, stand back."

Mrs. Eckles fixed her green eyes on the manual and *stared*. There was a small, blinding flash of blue light and a puff of yellow smoke. When that cleared, the manual had shrunk to the size of a matchbox. Taking his time, Bernard picked it up and opened it to the front page.

"Come on, come on," urged Mrs. Eckles. "What do I do?"

"You wait," said Bernard. "You wait until I'm good and ready." He reached into his pocket and took out a tiny pair of green-rimmed spectacles, which he placed on his nose.

"If those kids get in trouble, it's all your fault," said Mrs. Eckles fretfully. "You'll 'ave me to deal with then. What do I do?"

"Well, first you have to turn it on. Press the red button in the middle. No, no, not that one! The red one! RED! Oh, good grief, is it going to be like this all night?"

Mrs. Eckles's hovering finger landed on the correct button, more by luck than judgment, and the red light began winking on and off.

"Hey!" she said, pleased. "Now we're getting somewhere. Calm down, Bernard, I'm gettin' the hang of this. I remember now, we've got to wait while it does the thing with shoes."

"With sh—oh, I assume you mean *boots up*?"

"Boots, shoes, sandals, whatever. Carry on. Then what?"

"When the mist fills the glass, you move the third lever from the left to the right. That'll bring up a list of locations with the relevant map references. The green button activates the sound function. You have to speak clearly the name and address of the contactee then—"

"What?" interrupted Mrs. Eckles. "What did you say first off? What lever?"

"Third from the left! When the mist fills the glass, you move the third lever from the left to the right."

"What, this one?"

"No, no!" Bernard hopped up and down in alarm. "That's the second. That one's the volume. And whatever happens, don't touch the black button. There's a warning. Don't touch the black button unless you've turned the little blue knob all the way to the left or you'll lose the signal and have to start again."

"So which one is it again? The lever?"

"*The third from the left!* You have to move it to the right."

"This one?"

"No. Left. *Left.* Bit more. Not that much. Too far right. Back a bit. Now. NO! NOT THAT ONE! *THE THIRD FROM THE LEFT . . .*"

CHAPTER SIXTEEN

The Path Again

Clover lay spread-eagled on the Path with her eyes
screwed shut. At her side was the fallen tree. It had
missed her by a hairsbreadth.

"Clover? Are you all right? Speak to me! If you can't
speak, whistle. A short one for yes you're all right, a
long one if you're dead."

"Don't be ridiculous," Clover said, sighing. With a struggle, she opened her eyes. Wilf's anxious face was looming over her. Petula stood behind, peering over his shoulder. "Of course I'm not dead. If I was, the last thing I'd do is whistle at you. And do please stop stroking my hand."

Rather crossly, she pushed him away and scrambled to her feet.

"Here's your basket," said Petula, handing it over. "I'm afraid the sandwiches fell out and got a bit squashed." She pointed to an edge of oiled paper sticking out from beneath the fallen tree.

"Thanks," said Clover.

She stood, picking twigs out of her hair, staring thoughtfully at the tree, which lay across the path. It was a tall birch tree. Clearly, it was rotten to the core. There were no signs of ax marks. It hadn't been chopped down. It had just fallen. She put out a hand and gave it a poke. It felt like soggy cardboard.

"Why did you do that, exactly?" enquired Petula. "Run into the path of a falling tree?"

"I thought it was Pa," said Clover, "but it wasn't. It was a wolf, wearing his clothes. You saw it. A big bad wolf, like in the stories. It spoke to me. It said '*Timberrrrr!*'" She gave a little shiver. "Where is it now? Did it run away?"

Wilf and Petula exchanged a meaningful glance. Clover's eyes traveled from one to the other.

"Ohhh . . . " she said slowly. "Right. You didn't see it, did you?"

"No," said Wilf. "We didn't. We just saw you throw your arms up and run merrily under a falling tree."

"We didn't hear any chopping sounds, either," added Petula. "Wilf's right, there wasn't a wolf."

"I guess the Path made you think there was," said Wilf. "Like me on the rope bridge."

"Absolutely," agreed Petula. "An illusion."

"I'm an idiot," said Clover heavily.

"No, you're not," said Wilf.

"I am. I'm supposed to be the sensible one."

"You *are*. You were sensible enough to jump back just in time. Don't beat yourself up. Do you want a rest or are you ready to go on?"

"Of course I'm going on. Where's Philip Tidden?"

"Gone on up the Path, looking for water. He thought we might need it to bring you around."

"He shouldn't go off on his own," said Clover. "We've got to stick together. Supposing he falls in a bog or another tree comes down or . . ."

She broke off. Philip Tidden had appeared from the trees ahead and was waving and beckoning and giving the thumbs-up sign.

"Incredible!" marveled Petula. "Just like a horse. Horses sense water, you know."

The three of them stepped carefully over the tree and hurried on up the Path, where Philip Tidden eagerly waited.

"Are you all right?" he asked Clover.

"Fine," said Clover shortly.

"That's good. And I've got some more good news. There's a spring. Follow me, it's just over here."

He ducked under a low branch and plunged into the trees.

The spring was just a few paces away from the Path. It consisted of a sunken rock pool. Clear, cold water bubbled up from the middle. In fact, it was so cold that there were icicles all around the grass at the edge. Bushes with red berries on them clustered prettily around the pool. Their leaves were curiously shaped, like little drinking cups.

"You see?" said Philip Tidden, flushed with triumph. "Anyone fancy a drink? Clover?"

Clover looked longingly at the bubbling water. She felt thirstier than ever before.

"Mrs. Eckles said not to drink the water," she said uneasily.

"But it's fine," said Philip Tidden. "I've just filled my water bulb, it's really cold. Look." He fiddled in his pocket. A thin jet of water squirted sideways from his bow tie, catching Petula in the ear. "Sorry."

"No problem," said Petula kindly. "You keep practicing, Phil."

Philip Tidden snapped off one of the leaf cups, leaned over, dipped it in the water, raised it to his lips, and drank. "You see?" he said, smacking his lips. "It's lovely, really fresh—"

And then it happened. There was an eruption! The water churned, frothed, and rose in a great burst! Philip Tidden gave a startled yelp and tried to leap back. But to everyone's horror, something long and green with suckers came flashing out of the pool and wrapped itself around his wrist! The leaf cup shot from his hand and went spinning away—and he was jerked off his feet. His top half vanished below the bubbling surface, leaving his orange legs kicking desperately at the air.

There was more churning, and then, briefly, a head appeared. But it wasn't Philip Tidden's head.

It was a clown's head. Except that it didn't have a proper face. It had—a skull! A skull wearing a pointed white hat with a black pompom. Its eyes were dark sockets, and its grinning teeth were surrounded with a big painted red smile.

"LAUGHTER IS ALL," said the dark, spidery voice.

And the head went under.

"Quick!" howled Wilf. "Grab his legs!"

Clover and Petula sprang into action. They seized a leg each . . . and pulled. A shiny black shoe came off in Clover's hand, and Philip Tidden's flailing foot kicked her in the stomach. She grabbed for the leg again.

For a brief moment, Philip Tidden's startled head appeared above the surface in a bewildering confusion of froth and spray. Then it was gone. To add to the horror, the water had changed! It had become dark green, and a terrible smell rose from it.

"Pull!" yelled Wilf, leaping around in panic with his stick raised. "On three! One, two, three, puuuulllll!"

The girls pulled. They dug their heels in and strained backward . . . and slowly, bit by bit, Philip Tidden began to emerge. When his head finally appeared, it was green and dripping. His glasses dangled precariously from one ear. He was coughing and spluttering and gasping for air. His left arm was the last thing to emerge. Sadly, the tentacle was still wrapped around his wrist.

So Wilf brought down the stick. There was a horrible squishing sound as it connected with the tentacle.

"Grooooo-oooow!" choked Philip Tidden. But the tentacle maintained its grip.

So Wilf did it again. And again. All the while, Clover and Petula hauled on the legs. Poor Philip Tidden was being stretched like a bow string. But it was working. At each whack of the stick, the tentacle loosened its grip a little—and finally, at the fifth blow, it gave in. It just untwined itself and slithered away beneath the surface. Clover and Petula staggered backward, bringing Philip Tidden with them, and they all fell in a heap.

For a moment, the only sound was of panting and faint moans from Philip Tidden. And then Wilf spoke. Beneath his red hair, his face was pale. He said, "Let's not bother with a drink. Shall we go?"

He didn't need to suggest it twice.

★ ★ ★ ★ ★

It was a grim and silent party that walked along the Perilous Path. Nobody felt like talking. They all felt shaken up. Petula had her arm supportively around Philip Tidden's shoulders. He had tried to clean himself up with Clover's hanky, but it wasn't really up to the job. His top half was soaked and he smelled quite badly, although nobody mentioned it.

"Anyone fancy an apple?" said Petula suddenly.

Everyone stopped and stared at her.

"Are you serious?" said Wilf. "You've got apples?"

"Got a whole suitcase full," said Petula. "I've been saving them for Shorty."

"Mrs. Eckles said we shouldn't take any food offered us," said Clover doubtfully.

"Ah, but she didn't mean from a friend, did she?" argued Wilf. His mouth was watering already. "Petula's on our side. What's she going to do, poison us?"

"They might turn poisonous when we eat them," said Clover. "Or turn us into something . . . or . . . I don't know, have worms in. Who knows what the Path can do?"

"Trust me, they're fine," said Petula. "Look, I'll demonstrate."

She knelt down, clicked open her suitcase, and lifted the lid. It was indeed full of rosy apples. Petula selected a big one and bit into it.

"See? Go on, help yourselves."

Wilf and Philip Tidden took an apple each. After a moment's hesitation, Clover did too. She bit into it. It tasted wonderful.

All four stood crunching and chewing and thinking about what had just happened while the juice ran down their chins.

"Petula," said Wilf, crunching. "I'm really sorry about what I said earlier, about you not being interesting. I see the point of you now. You're here to help with the rescue and keep our spirits up and feed us apples."

"That's right," said Philip Tidden. He gave a rare smile. "She's an asset, like me."

"You don't think Herby went near that horrible spring, do you?" said Clover. "I just couldn't bear it if he—he saw that—that—"

"Nah," said Wilf, a bit too quickly. "Who needs water if you've got sweets? He's still up ahead, mark my words."

"Of course he is," said Philip Tidden.

"Absolutely," agreed Petula. A little silence fell. Then Clover said, suddenly, "How many?"

"How many what?" asked Wilf.

"How many Perils so far?"

"Um . . . four, I think. No, five if you count Old Barry."

Philip Tidden and Petula looked at each other and shrugged. Old Barry was news to them.

"Barry," pondered Clover. "Then Clown College and the Academy and the Wolf and the . . . Thing in the rock pool. You're right, that's five. What about you try-ing to throw yourself off the bridge, though. Should that count?"

"I don't know," said Wilf shortly. Did she have to bring that up again? "Why do you ask, anyway?"

"Because the saying says seven."

"What saying?"

"Mrs. Eckles told it to me. *Woe! Seven Times Woe Betide All Ye Who Walk the Perilous Path*. That might mean there are only two more to go."

"It might," said Wilf. "But we can't count on it."

"It makes sense, though. What next, I wonder? Attack by birds? Lured over a precipice? A gingerbread cottage? What? Oh, I *wish* Mrs. Eckles were here to help us!"

"Still nothing from the mirror, I suppose?" asked Wilf without much hope.

Clover reached into her basket, took out the mirror, tapped it, and waved it around a bit.

"What are you doing?" asked Petula.

"Waiting for Mrs. Eckles to get through, " explained Clover. "The Witch I was telling you about. She's trying to contact us on a Crystal Ball, but I guess she's having trouble." She put the mirror back in her basket. "So, we're still on our own."

"We're a team now, though," said Philip Tidden.

"Absolutely," said Petula. "A winning team, right?"

"Certainly we are," said Wilf. "And if Clover's right, there's only two more perils. Bring 'em on, I say!"

And they moved on up the Path.

CHAPTER SEVENTEEN

A Lot of Shouting

Back at the castle, Miss Fly and Mesmeranza stood facing each other across the turret room.

"So let me get this straight, Fly," said Mesmeranza. "Someone whose name you can't remember tells you that they've heard a rumor that a dear little stray orphan kitten has been seen hanging around the Hunting Lodge in a pine forest over twenty miles away. Yes?"

"Yes," said Miss Fly with a gulp.

"And so you were *worried* about the poor diddums."

"Well, yes."

"So you took it upon yourself to fly to the rescue on Booboo, although you know you need my written permission."

"Well, it was an emergency. . . ."

"You land. You search. You call. You make a noise like a fish head. But there is no orphaned kitten."

"Not that I saw, no. And I didn't make a noise like a f—"

"You decide to make inquiries at the Lodge. Much to your amazement, the Lodge appears to be deserted."

"Yes. I told you, there was a note saying *closed.*"

"While standing there, puzzled and perplexed, a strange noise comes to your ears. You race to the side and are just in time to see my chief huntsman and his two brothers making off into the blue on a loaded cart. "

"Exactly."

"Lucky you were there, eh?"

"Yes, wasn't it?"

"Fly," said Mesmeranza. "That is a ludicrous stream of lies." She withdrew an envelope from the folds of her gown and waved it triumphantly under Miss Fly's nose.

"See this? Brought to me by the groom, who isn't as stupid as he looks. It's the letter, Fly. The *vital black-mail letter that was to set the whole thing in motion*."

"Oh my!" Miss Fly clapped a hand to her brow. "My brain! I knew I posted something, but it must have been the vet's bill!"

"Oh, *really*? Do you know what I think, Fly? I have a theory. My theory is this. *The child was never kidnapped in the first place.* Plainly, you are in league with the huntsman. The two of you colluded to foil my Plan and split the gold between you."

"We did not!" protested Miss Fly, genuinely shocked. "I would *never* do that!"

"No? You're always complaining I don't pay you enough."

"Well, yes, but . . . in league with the *huntsman*? That's ridiculous."

"I'm not a fool, Fly. You offered him a caring glass of iced tea."

"He was *hot*!"

"For all I know, the two of you are planning to elope together."

"This is preposterous!" twittered Miss Fly. "Me and the huntsman! As if . . . as if I'd ever . . . preposterous!"

"You couldn't wait to hand over the gold, could you?

I wondered why you were so eager. Now I see it's to pay for the honeymoon. Don't deny it, Fly. It won't do you any good."

"But you've got it all *wrong*! Look, all right. There was no kitten . . . I admit it, I went to check on the child. I was concerned about his living conditions. But he wasn't *there*. Not in the cart, not in the Lodge. It came as a complete surprise. I don't know *where* he is."

"But I do," said Mesmeranza smugly.

"You do?" Miss Fly blinked in surprise.

"I do. While you were out poking your dripping nose into my affairs like some kind of demented social worker, I received a call from Ida Dismal. It seems that the wretched child has most inconveniently wandered off down the Perilous Path."

"The what?"

"Fly, you have worked for me for more years than I care to count. Are you telling me I have never mentioned the Perilous Path?"

"You talk a lot," said Miss Fly, defensively. "I can't be expected to remember everything you say. Is it *very* perilous? Is the child in danger?"

"Of course he's in danger! The clue's in the name! On a Perilous Path, there are likely to be *perils*, don't you think? But that's not the point. The point is, he's

214

supposed to be in danger from *me*. Anyway, I don't have time to stand here talking to you. I'm through with delegating to underlings. I shall find the brat myself. Find him and bring him back here. Then the Plan shall proceed as before, despite your incompetence, disloyalty, downright treachery, and sickening sentimentality. Never fear, Fly, that Book will be mine. And woe betide anyone who tries to stand in my way."

"Don't look at me," said Miss Fly. "*I'm* not stopping you. But . . ." Her voice trailed off.

"But what?"

"I was just thinking. Supposing you don't find him first? There must be a lot of people looking for him. His family. Neighbors. The local Witches. Your own sister."

"Nonsense. We are talking about the *Perilous Path*, Fly. An old, magical, wicked way that comes and goes at will, not the road leading to the local chip shop. There's a saying Grandmother taught us. '*Woe! Seven Times Woe Betide All Ye Who Walk the Perilous Path!*'"

"I've never heard that one," said Miss Fly. "My grandma always said, '*Be Kind to Cats.*'"

"Which is why I ended up as a powerful Witch and you ended up as my slave."

"I'm a secretary, not a slave," said Miss Fly with a

sniff. "Anyway, please yourself. If you want to put yourself in peril, that's your affair."

"Fly," said Mesmeranza. "Get it into your thick head. I *am* peril. Out of my way! I'm off to get that child!"

★ ★ ★ ★ ★

Back at the cottage, dawn was breaking outside. From inside came the sound of a breaking teacup. Mrs. Eckles had just thrown it at the wall, in a fit of mad frustration. *"Make up your mind, you pesky little twerp!"* she bellowed. "This lever, that lever, this button, that button—how am I supposed to work it out when you go so *flippin' fast!"*

"It's because you don't *listen!"* raged Bernard. His skin had gone a weird shade of greenish purple, like that of a ripening plum. He was stabbing at the instruction manual with a webbed finger and stamping his foot. "I'm telling you clearly. Just do as I say!"

"I did! Then you said I was doin' it wrong!"

"That's because you were! Every time I say left you go right, and when I tell you to press the red one, you press the green!"

"Yes, well, it's all too bloomin' complicated. Where's the on and off switch, that's all I want to know!"

"There isn't one!"

"Well there should be!"

"A bad workman always blames his tools," sneered Bernard. "There's nothing wrong with the Ball. It's you."

"Oh, *is* it?"

"Yes. Modern magical technology is *sophisticated* . . ."

The argument would have probably gone on in this way forever. But just at that moment, there came a thunderous knocking at the door.

"Now what!" snapped Mrs. Eckles. "Who's comin' here pesterin' at this time o' day?"

She stood up, went to the door, and snatched it open. Bernard moved to the edge of his shelf and craned forward, trying to see who was there, but the cupboard was at the wrong angle. There came the sounds of muffled conversation. Then the sound of the door closing, and Mrs. Eckles came marching back. There was an expression on her face that was hard to read.

"What?" said Bernard.

"News," said Mrs. Eckles. "Important news that changes everythin'. That does it. I'm through with messin' about. This thing is gonna *work*!"

She plopped down at the table and fixed her green gaze on the Ballmaster Multidimensional Mark Six, which just sat there, being generally unhelpful. The little wisp of gray mist twisted and turned in the glass, and the little red light on the black base was on. It was gently buzzing. That was all.

Mrs. Eckles shot out her hands and pressed every single button at random. She flicked switches and roughly pulled levers any old way. Bernard winced as colored lights flickered on and off. The misty gray wisp began spinning around, and a sudden puff of black smoke came from somewhere under the base.

"There!" snapped Mrs. Eckles. "That should do somethin'!"

It did.

EEEEEEEEEEEEEEEEEEEEEEEEEEEE . . .

CHAPTER EIGHTEEN

A Sighting!

"It's no good," announced Wilf. "We've got to sit down."

They had been trudging along for some time now. Exhaustion was taking its toll. Wilf's blisters were back with a vengeance. Clover's boots were pinching too, and her face was grim. Even Petula had lost some of her cheerfulness. Philip Tidden walked a few paces ahead, aware that no one wanted him too close because of his horrible old-pondy smell, which showed no signs of going away. It appeared that sympathy for him had run out. The Path was getting to them. Little arguments kept breaking out.

"We can't stop," snapped Clover. "Herby'll get farther away."

"Well, he's got to rest sometime," pointed out Wilf reasonably. "He's only little. His legs must be tired too."

"I know that! Don't you think I know that? Of course I know his legs are tired!"

"Calm down, grumpy, I'm just saying. No need to snap."

"Well, stop going on about tired little legs, then!"

"I'm not going on. I'm just saying we need a rest."

"You can rest if you like, but I'm not. He's my brother and he's sad and scared and alone, and I'm not stopping until I find him. Come on, Petula, let's go."

Whether Petula would have sided with Clover or Wilf we will never know, because at that point, Philip Tidden began shouting and beckoning.

"He's found something!" exclaimed Petula. "I do believe he's done it again! That boy has real talent."

Philip Tidden was a short way up the Path, examining a patch of grass where there lay a fallen log . . . and scattered beneath were a number of sweet wrappers! And not only that. On the log itself was a rough, scribbled drawing of a stick man in red chalk!

"More clues," said Philip Tidden, looking proud but modest at the same time. "It looks like he sat down here and had a rest. Ate some sweets and did a little drawing."

"He won't win any prizes for art," said Wilf, "but he's getting through the sweets pretty quickly. He might be sad and scared but there's nothing wrong with his appetite."

"I suppose you're hoping he leaves some for you," said Clover. But she grinned as she said it. After all, this was good news. For the first time in ages, her spirits lifted.

"How long ago was he here, I wonder?" pondered Petula.

"No telling," said Wilf. "Could be hours ago."

"No," said Philip Tidden, slowly. "It wasn't."

He raised his arm and pointed. Everyone turned and looked.

Far up ahead, at the point where the Path vanished into the trees, stood a tiny figure. It was too far away to make out details . . . but there was no mistaking the red woolly hat and the cut-down flour sack with the red pocket.

"Herby!" screamed Clover. "It's Herby!"

"Wait!" shouted Wilf. "It might not be! Watch out, it could be another illusion . . ."

But Clover was already running.

Up ahead, the small figure appeared to hesitate . . . and then, to everyone's amazement, it turned its back and scampered off.

Wilf, Philip Tidden, and Petula glanced at each other, and with one accord took off after Clover.

"Herby! Come back!" cried Clover. "It's me!"

"Herby!" bawled Wilf, wincing as he hobbled along on his blistered feet. "Stop! It's us!"

But Herby didn't stop. If anything, he increased his speed.

"What's the matter with him?" panted Clover. "Why isn't he stopping? *Herby, you bad boy! Come here this minute, I'm not playing now!*"

Herby showed no signs of slowing down. But he had short little legs. The distance between him and his pursuers was steadily decreasing.

"We're gaining!" gasped Petula. "Come on, faster!"

It didn't seem possible to run any faster, but somehow, they did. Clover was in the lead, followed by Wilf, then Petula. Philip Tidden was lagging behind somewhat because of trouser problems, but he gamely kept going.

"Herby!" shouted Clover. "Stop messing about! This isn't a game!" Herby was just ahead of them now. His little legs were going like pistons and they could hear his gasping breath.

Clover stretched out her arm to catch him. The first time she missed, but on the second try she managed to grab a handful of sack. Herby was brought up short. Caught off-balance, he veered to one side and went crashing down headfirst, bringing Clover with him. They rolled over into a shallow ditch. Instantly, Herby was up on his hands and knees, attempting to crawl off into the bushes—but Clover was ready for him. She grabbed for the sack again, took a firm hold, flipped him over, all ready to smother him with kisses—and almost died of shock!

It wasn't Herby. The face she was looking at was pinched and ferocious. It had vicious black eyes, a sharp nose, and a mouth full of wicked little teeth. The mouth opened to bite her. Before it could, Wilf grabbed it by the scruff of the neck and lifted it into the air. It hung there, emitting enraged little hisses, legs paddling.

Numb with disappointment, Clover took Philip Tidden's hand and scrambled out of the ditch.

"What is it?" asked Petula, curious. "Some sort of . . . *gnome* or something?"

"Haven't a clue," said Wilf. "But I'll soon find out." He gave the newcomer a rough little shake. "Stop spitting, you, and tell us who you are!"

"Pssssssssst!" hissed the little creature. *"I ssssspit in your eye! No gnome! Goblin! Bad boy, leggo!"* It twisted its neck, trying desperately to sink its teeth into Wilf's hand.

Wilf brandished his stick. "Want me to use this?"

"Ahhhh! No! Not ssssstick!" shrieked the Goblin. It went into a frenzied panic, thrashing its arms around and kicking its legs. Wilf nearly dropped it.

"What are you doing in Herby's clothes?" demanded Clover. Furiously, she reached out and plucked the red hat from the goblin's head. Two huge, pointed ears sprung out. They did nothing to add to its beauty.

"No do nuttin'! Not ssssssstick!"

"Talk, then," roared Wilf, right into the goblin's face. "You stole these clothes from him, didn't you? Where is he? What have you done with him?"

"No do nuttin'!"

"You did! You took his sweets, too, didn't you? And his chalk! Fancy robbing a poor little kid, you lying, bullying, disgusting little mugger!"

"There's nothing worse than a bully," remarked Petula. "You tell him, Wilf."

"Search the pocket, Phil," said Wilf. "Let's see what else he's got."

"Who, me? Wow. All right," said Philip Tidden, pleased to be included. He moved toward the goblin, who gave another little scream and cringed.

But just then, something happened that surprised everybody. It wasn't a good thing. In fact, it was the worst thing that anyone could have imagined.

From overhead, there came the beating of mighty wings, followed by the cracking sound of breaking branches. Leaves and twigs rained down. Everyone automatically ducked and threw their arms over their heads. The goblin slithered from Wilf's grasp, landed on all fours, and shot off hissing into the undergrowth.

There was a great, thumping crash . . . and suddenly, the world was full of flying horse! It was rearing and lashing the air with its wings. And on its broad, sweating back sat . . .

"Mesmeranza," Clover said with a groan. "Oh, no. That's all we need."

There she was . . . a vision in a purple hooded riding cloak with matching gloves. Purple high heels were jammed into the stirrups.

"Wow!" Petula gasped, starting forward. "A horse with wings! How absolutely *super*! What a splendid creature!"

"Watch it," said Wilf, pulling her back from the flapping wings and flying hooves. "It's Booboo, and it's evil!"

"Nonsense. No such thing as a bad horse, just irresponsible owners. I cannot believe that woman is wearing those shoes." She raised her voice and shouted. "Those shoes are absolutely unsuitable for riding! I shall report you to the Pony Club!"

Booboo stopped rearing and flapping and came down on all fours. His ears had pricked up at these unexpected words of support. He didn't have many admirers. For once, someone was on his side. He tossed his head in agreement, tucked his wings away tidily, and stood quiet as a lamb, hoping for more. Petula clucked to him soothingly, and said, "There's a good horse."

Mesmeranza ignored her and began to dismount. Booboo considered kicking her but decided against it. His new champion was watching him, and he wanted her approval.

"Well now," purred Mesmeranza. "Just look at this! We meet again, Clover Twig. And on the Perilous Path, of all places. You're not as tidy as usual, dear. Has it been giving you a *very* hard time?"

"As if you care," said Clover.

"Now, now. Let's not get off on the wrong foot. I see you have young Master Wilfred Brownswoody in tow. Lovely to see you again, Wilf. And what have we here? Two *new* friends. Some sort of trampy clown and a loony horse lover. Quite a little party."

"Look," said Clover tiredly, "I don't know why you're here and I'm not interested. If you're planning to steal the cottage again, go and argue about it with Mrs. Eckles."

"Oh, I'm not after the cottage anymore, darling. I have other fish to fry."

"Then go and fry them."

"Dear, dear." Mesmeranza shook her head. "Always so stubborn and rude. You don't change. Now, what would you be doing here, I wonder? Let me guess." She tilted her head to one side and tapped her chin. "Oh, *I* know. You're looking for your poor, lost little brother, right?"

"None of your business what we're doing," said Wilf.

"Wrong," said Mesmeranza. "*So* wrong. Leave my horse alone, girl!"

Petula had strolled over to Booboo and was stroking his nose. Philip Tidden appeared to have given up following the conversation and was whistling under his breath, kicking his heels with his hands in his pockets.

"What exactly are you talking about?" asked Wilf.

"It may come as a surprise," said Mesmeranza, "but it so happens that I am also after the wretched brat. What it all comes down to is who gets to him first. I have a flying horse at my disposal, plus I intend to prevent you from looking any further, so I *rather* think it will be me."

"What do you want with Herby?" demanded Clover. "What's he got to do with you?"

"Ah. Well, he's the bait, you see. The bait that tempts the fish. The fish being *you*, darling."

"So you're intending to kidnap Herby just to spite me?"

"Oh, don't flatter yourself. It's far more complicated than that. I have a task for you. It's all part of my latest Plan. You should have had a letter telling you all this, but there were unexpected postal delays. Basically, I want the Bad Spell Book."

"The what?"

"Don't pretend you don't know what I'm talking about. Grandmother's Bad Spell Book is hidden in the cottage. Demelza has it."

"She's never said anything to me," said Clover with a shrug.

"Well, I know it's there. Grandmother told me. It's under a loose slab in the kitchen."

"No, it's not. I fixed the loose slab, and there's no stupid book under it."

"You're lying."

"No, I'm not. But even if there *was* such a book, which there isn't, you can't get at it because you're forbidden to cross the threshold unless Mrs. Eckles invites you."

"I am aware of that. That's why you will bring it out to me. No Book, no brother. That's the Plan. You must agree, it's rather clever."

Clover opened her mouth to let fly with another cutting remark, then closed it again. Something had caught her attention.

Her basket was vibrating! From under the cloth, there came a faint buzzing noise. Would Wilf hear it too?

"You know, it *is* rather clever, actually," said Wilf loudly, catching Clover's eye. The buzzing was faint. If he kept talking, maybe Mesmeranza wouldn't notice. "I've got to hand it to you. Could you run it past us again? I'd just like to get it straight in my head. I'm sure the others would like to hear, even if Clover doesn't."

"By all means," said Mesmeranza graciously. "In fact, let me start from the beginning. Grandmother had this book, you see. We called it her Bad Spell Book. I confess I had forgotten all about it until . . ."

The buzzing sound was becoming more urgent. Slowly, cautiously, Clover moved her hand under the cloth and felt around for the mirror. And then there came a crackling, followed by a tiny, distorted voice calling her name.

"Clover? Are you there? Pick up, will you? It's me, I've gotten through!"

CHAPTER NINETEEN

Mrs. Eckles Gets Through

"Ah," said Mrs. Eckles. "Now we're gettin' somewhere. I've gotten through."

"You have?" gasped Bernard.

He couldn't believe it. With his own eyes, he had
watched Mrs. Eckles do every single thing she wasn't
supposed to do. Pulled every lever the wrong way in

the wrong order and pressed every button any old how, causing the Ballmaster Multidimensional Mark Six to crackle, smoke, flash colored lights, and finally burst into that awful, earsplitting screech. Remember it?

EEEEEEEEEEEEEEEEEEEEE . . .

Neville had flattened his ears, backed away, and fled upstairs. Even Bernard had retreated behind a jar with his hands pressed over his ears.

But this time, Mrs. Eckles held her ground. She simply planted her fists on the table and fixed her eyes on the screeching Ball.

"Right," she announced. "I've had it with you. Here's the thing. You've got a choice. Either you pack it in and put me through to Clover or . . ." She leaned forward and whispered something. Then sat back and said, "And that's worse than a fryin' pan."

. . . *EEEEeeeek!*

The screech cut off. Quickly and efficiently, one by one, the flashing lights winked out, leaving only the little red one. The black clouds of smoke cleared away, leaving only the dainty little wisp of mist drifting about inside the Crystal Ball.

Amazingly, unbelievably, despite all that abuse and mishandling . . . the Ballmaster Multidimensional Mark Six was working!

"See?" said Mrs. Eckles, triumphantly. "That's the way to do it."

"What do you see?" asked Bernard faintly.

"Got a close-up of inside the basket. Good quality wicker, I must say. *Sssh*, stay quiet now, I don't want no interruptions. *Clover? Are you there? Pick up, will you? It's me, I've gotten through!*"

Inside the Crystal, the ghostly twist vanished. There was a dizzying, flickering effect—and suddenly, Clover's face swam into view. She looked pale, Mrs. Eckles thought. Pale and tired. Not herself, by any means.

"There you are!" said Mrs. Eckles. "Sorry I took so long, coupla technical hitches; you can blame Bernard. I got news. I just had a visit from—"

"Mrs. Eckles," interrupted Clover, speaking urgently under her breath. "Listen. We're in trouble."

"What sort o' trouble?"

"I'm turning the mirror around. See for yourself."

There was another confused effect as a hundred images flashed by, then settled.

A strange scene met Mrs. Eckles's eyes. Several figures were gathered on a long, straight Path that cut between too-green trees. She knew Wilf, of course, but there were two others she didn't recognize—a small boy in a filthy clown suit and a girl in riding breeches, who appeared to be feeding apples to an unusually calm but all too familiar horse.

And there was someone else. Someone who didn't look calm at all. Someone who was striding up and down in a pair of unsuitable purple high heels, waving her arms around, talking animatedly.

"Oh," said Mrs. Eckles slowly. "Right. This I wasn't expectin'. Bernard! Emergency overdrive!"

"What? I can't do that, you know I can't do that! This is an old cottage; it has to be handled careful—"

"Emergency overdrive! *Now!*"

★ ★ ★ ★ ★

Back on the Path, Mesmeranza was really getting into her stride.

". . . make it rain snakes, turn the footmen into giant lizards, cause a plague of flying cockroaches, anything I like. Once I get my hands on that Book. Mislaying the bait has complicated matters somewhat, but a slight glitch in my Plan isn't—" She broke off. "What are you doing with that mirror?"

"Nothing," said Clover with a shrug. She smoothed her hair and slipped the mirror back in her basket. "Just bored, that's all. Bored of hearing you talk. All you ever do is strut around talking and threatening people. You think it's all about you, but it isn't. I'm sick of listening."

"Insolent girl!" hissed Mesmeranza. "How *dare* you speak to me like that!" From beneath her cloak, she produced a thin black stick. "Remember this? Grandmother's wand! All charged up and ready to go. Remember what it's like to be on the receiving end? You'll recall it packs quite a punch. "

"I thought your grandmother took it back," said Wilf. "I distinctly remember her taking it off you and going off to the Twilight Home with it."

"Yes, well, now it's mine again. Don't move, any of you! I'm just debating what to do. Turn you into pillars of stone or zap you into next week. Each has a certain charm."

"Excuse me?" said Philip Tidden, suddenly and unexpectedly. "Is that a joke wand?"

"I beg your pardon?"

"Your wand. Is it made of rubber?"

"*Rubber?*"

"It's just that in Clown College, all weapons are made of rubber. Could I take a look?"

"Stand back!" ordered Mesmeranza as Philip Tidden moved toward her, hands in his pockets. "Not another step!"

"All right," said Philip Tidden. "Watch this, Wilf. I think I've got the knack now."

Whooosh!

A thin jet of foul-smelling water shot from the center of his bow tie and squirted Mesmeranza in the left eye. At exactly the same time, Wilf ran forward, stepped to the side, and swiped at the back of her knees with his stick. Simultaneously, a perfectly aimed apple came whizzing through the air and connected sharply with her ear. Mesmeranza gave a little scream, clawed at her eye, clutched at her head, and buckled at the knees, dropping the wand, which fell under a bush.

"Get it, Clover!" shouted Wilf.

Clover dropped her basket, made a dive for the bush, and snatched up the wand. Instantly, an unpleasant buzzing sensation crackled up her arm. At the same time, Mesmeranza rolled over, shot out a long arm, and seized her by the wrist. Long red talons dug in. Clover gave a sharp cry of pain, her fingers loosened, and the wand once again fell in the dirt. Snarling, Mesmeranza kicked out with a high-heeled shoe, catching Clover in the stomach. Clover reeled back, winded. Mesmeranza reached for the fallen wand . . .

And then something else happened. Once again, there came the sound of breaking branches overhead, followed by an almighty, earth-shattering thump from behind. The ground shook violently. Cracks appeared at their feet. Everyone whirled around, fearing the worst.

There, sitting right across the Path, was the flying cottage. It sat in a great cloud of swirling dust, surrounded by fallen trees and broken glass from the shattered windows.

As if that wasn't dramatic enough, there came the sound of shouting voices, and from out of the trees poured . . .

"The gardeners!" said Petula with a gasp. "They've come to get me!"

They had. A whole posse of them, armed with rakes and shovels. They all wore straw hats and rolled-up pants and were shaking their fists!

The back door of the cottage burst open, and Mrs. Eckles appeared in the doorway.

"Quick!" she shouted. "Over the threshold! Now!"

Nobody needed telling twice. All four of them reached for each other's hands and raced for the open door.

"In! In!" squawked Mrs. Eckles as they fell into the kitchen. "Back away from the door! I'll deal with this." And she folded her arms and stood waiting in the doorway.

Mesmeranza stood, wand in hand. Shaking with fury, she strode toward the cottage, green eyes blazing. But she stopped well short of the threshold.

The gardeners stopped shouting and fist waving. This was clearly Witch business. They stood around uncertainly, scratching their heads.

"You again!" snapped Mrs. Eckles. "I thought I'd

seen the last of you, but here you are, turnin' up like a bad penny, givin' everyone a load o' grief! I suppose you're after somethin', as usual. What is it this time?"

"She's planning to kidnap Herby!" Wilf piped up helpfully. "Something about some old book. She's trying to make Clover steal it for her."

"Silence, boy!" rasped Mesmeranza. "Nobody asked you to speak. This is between me and my sister."

"You're dead right it is," snorted Mrs. Eckles. "Time you picked on someone yer own size. And if you're referrin' to that old book of wicked spells that Grandmother put under the loose slab, you're wastin' yer time. That's long gone. I burned it."

"*What?*" Mesmeranza's jaw dropped.

"You heard me. There's enough bad stuff already in the world without that fallin' into the wrong hands. By which I mean yours . . ."

"*You're lying!*"

"Nope, it's the truth. But I ain't going to stand here arguin' with you. I need to get these kids 'ome. Looks like they've 'ad a rough time of it. By the way, I'll be mentionin' to Grandmother that you stole 'er wand. I expect you'll be hearin' from 'er. Wouldn't want to be in your shoes."

And with that, Mrs. Eckles slammed the door. From

outside came a scream of rage, followed by a whoosh as a stream of green light arced from the tip of the wand and thumped harmlessly into the wood. The gardeners dropped their rakes and shovels and dived for the bushes.

"Don't worry, Protection Spells'll cope," said Mrs. Eckles calmly. "Right, Bernard, take 'er up, on the double."

"Wait!" shouted Clover. "What about Herby? We haven't found him, he's still on the Path!"

"No, he ain't," said Mrs. Eckles. "He's back 'ome with yer ma, safe and sound."

Clover, Wilf, Philip Tidden, and Petula stared at her in disbelief.

"*What?*"

"Yep. Your grampy came to tell me, Wilf. Seems he was never on the Path to start with."

"But you said . . ."

"Yeah, yeah, I know I did. Thought I saw 'im on the bridge, but I musta been mistaken. Seems the peddler and Tilly Adams found 'im in the woods, cryin' and shiverin' in 'is undershirt. They was on the way back from their weddin', all set to make peace with Tilly's pa. Gave 'im a lift 'ome in the cart."

"So, what you're saying is," said Wilf slowly, "we went through all that *for nothing?*"

"'Fraid so. Still. No bones broken, eh? And you made a coupla new friends. Plus, you survived the Perilous Path, not many can say that. Now, let's get off it, before I starts turnin' nasty. Hold on tight, we're goin' up!"

Over in the cupboard, Bernard blew on the bubble . . . and the cottage went up!

Epilogue

That would be a good place to end, don't you think? After all, what could be a better ending than a magic cottage flying dramatically to the rescue just when everything seems lost?

But there are a few things you will want to know, and who can blame you? Let's tie up some loose ends and see if it all worked out neatly.

THE JOURNEY HOME

If you want to know about the journey home, it went smoothly. It took a while because Bernard was still a bit shaky from taking the cottage into overdrive and couldn't cope with more speeding. Philip Tidden and Petula were terribly excited, running from window to window, because flying was all new to them. Wilf just stood with his back to the wall, groaning and suffering from vertigo, as usual. Clover found the broom and swept up the pieces of shattered cup that Mrs. Eckles had thrown at the wall, then made everyone a cup of tea. Mrs. Eckles complained that it wasn't sweet enough. They all talked a lot, of course. There was a lot of filling in of gaps to do.

GOOD-BYE TO NEW FRIENDS

How did Philip Tidden and Petula get home? The cottage dropped them off at dawn—first Petula, then Philip Tidden. As expected, Petula lived in a grand house with enormous grounds. The cottage swooped down and hovered just over the lawn. Petula clapped Wilf on the back, shot Philip Tidden a cheery thumbs-up, gave Clover a hug, and said, "I'll write, absolutely."

"Will he make you go back? Your pops?" asked Clover.

"Not a chance. I can wind him around my little finger," said Petula and hopped down. The last they saw of her was a tiny figure, jauntily waving before making for the stables.

Philip Tidden's house turned out to be a small, dull bungalow in a small, dull town. The lace curtains were firmly drawn, but Philip Tidden said his mother and father would be in for the simple reason that they never went out. The minute garden was too small for the cottage to land, so he had to climb down a tree. He managed quite nimbly, though. Everyone agreed that he had greatly grown in confidence. The last they saw of him, he was checking the angle of his tie and filling his pocket bulb from the water feature before going in to bring lasting fun and happiness to his parents. He promised to write too, and I think he will.

THREATS AND GROVELING

You may want to know what Mrs. Eckles whispered to the Ballmaster Multidimensional Mark Six. Well, that's really a Witch secret—although the words "throw" and "deep well" and "forever" might give you a clue. She took it back to Granny Dismal the next day, with a humble air and a bunch of bright red peonies from the garden. She said words like "can't thank you enough," and "really, *really* sorry," and "worked perfectly, wonderful gadget," and "eternally grateful." Granny Dismal looked it over and couldn't find a single scratch. It seemed in perfect working order, too. Even faster, if anything. Grudgingly, she accepted the apologies and said words like "understand it was an emergency," and "glad it all turned out all right," and even "suppose you can borrow it again, if you must." Mrs. Eckles's reply to that included the words "very kind," followed quickly by "but," "no," and "thanks." They parted with promises to meet up at the next potluck dinner, but neither of them meant it. Granny Dismal waited until Mrs. Eckles had gone before flinging the flowers in the compost because they weren't gray.

WHAT ABOUT MESMERANZA?

Of course, you will want to find out what happened to Mesmeranza, whom we left in a right old tizzy, firing off useless lightning bolts on the Perilous Path, her Plan finally in ruins. All I know is that she hasn't arrived back at the castle, so she's probably still there. As we know, the Path has a bad effect on Witches, so who knows what she will be like on her return. If she *does* return, that is.

At any rate, Booboo came flying home without her, in a strangely good mood for once, smelling strongly of apples. Of his rider, no sign. Even Miss Fly doesn't know where she is. She is in no hurry to make inquiries and is taking full advantage of the time off. Things are a lot more relaxed around the place, and she is able to give her full attention to the cats.

GOLD

Did Humperdump Chunk get his bag of gold? No. That would be ridiculous. A whole bag of gold, just for giving a few directions? I don't think so. When he tried reminding Miss Fly, she explained that she never actually *promised* him gold, just asked him what he thought of it, which is a different thing altogether. Rather sly for Miss Fly, but let's face it, he didn't deserve it. At least he now knows for sure that she doesn't love him. He can move on.

What about Hybrow Hunter and his brothers? Did *they* get away with the gold? Did they spend it all on riotous living, with chicken drumsticks and jugs of ale served by rosy-cheeked maidens? No. They bought their old mother a house and fixed it up rather nicely. The rest was invested in a logging company, which is doing very well. They seem to have turned over a new leaf, so that's good.

HERBY, WILF, AND CLOVER

And Little Herby? He is absolutely fine. In fact, let's find out for ourselves. Mrs. Eckles has given Clover an extra day off to spend at home, which is only fair. Unlike Wilf. Not only didn't he get a day off, he got a telling off from Old Trowzer about Mrs. Pluck's missing loaf and eggs, which seems unfair, but there you have it. After only two hours' sleep, he is reluctantly off to deliver a replacement, but has stopped in to see Clover on the way. Tell you what. Let's pop in on them one last time.

IN THE GARDEN

"You'd never think he'd been mugged by a goblin, would you?" said Wilf to Clover. "Not to look at him."

They both stood in the garden, staring at Little Herby. He wore his spare cut-down flour sack, which didn't have a pocket, and was happily handing nails to Pa, who was fixing the garden gate. His newly washed red hat was on his head, and he was tunelessly singing a song about a chicken. Pa's back didn't seem to be too bad. He was swigging from a mug of tea, even joining in the chorus.

"He's fine," agreed Clover. "Hasn't even mentioned it. Seems to have taken it all in stride. He was most excited about getting a lift home in the peddler's cart. He got more free chalk and a squeaky toy. Does nothing but scribble and squeak all day. He hasn't mentioned his comfort rag, either. I don't know where that went."

"I reckon there's a lot of things we'll never know about his little adventures."

"It's my guess the goblin jumped him just before he started up the Path," said Clover. "Took his clothes and stuff and left him crying. And then the peddler found him. I can't believe we were following a false trail all that time."

"I can't believe we were only away for a night. It seemed to take forever on the Path."

"So many Perils in so short a time," agreed Clover.

"It doesn't seem possible. Were there seven? I keep trying to work it out."

"Who cares?" said Wilf. "It's all over now. And we won, didn't we?"

"Yes," said Clover. "We did. We won."

And they looked at each other and grinned.

I think we'll leave them there, before Wilf drops the loaf in the dirt again and spoils it all.

And that really is the end. Except . . .

ONE LAST THING

You may want to know if Clover ate that last sweet. Remember? The blue one rolling around in the bottom of her basket?

Sadly, no. When she looked for it, it was gone. Maybe somebody took it, or maybe she just lost it. Of course, she's far too sensible to mind that much. It was only a sweet. But when she lies down at night in her little attic room at Mrs. Eckles's cottage, she likes to imagine how it might have tasted.

KAYE UMANSKY

© Middleton Mann

What did you want to be when you grew up?
A circus high-wire artist, in pink spangles. Fearlessly hurling myself through the air. Silly, really, because I'm scared of heights.

Were you a reader or a non-reader growing up?
A huge reader. My family didn't have much money. The library was free.

When did you realize you wanted to be a writer?
It was something I always did, for fun. I wrote little stories and songs and made up plays and kept a diary. I didn't try to get published until I was nearly forty years old.

What's your most embarrassing childhood memory?
Falling down in the snow in front of a load of teenage boys waiting at a bus stop. My school skirt split up the side. Argh. I don't want to think about it.

What's your favorite childhood memory?
Singing carols around the piano with my family.

What was your favorite thing about school?
Leaving at four o'clock.

What was your least favorite thing about school?
Bullies. I came across a lot of them.

What were your hobbies as a kid? What are your hobbies now?
My mum was a music teacher, so I did a lot of singing and piano practice. These days, I listen to a lot of music. All different kinds. And I read a great deal.

Do you have any siblings?
No siblings. I am an only child. I think being on my own a lot kicked off my writing habit, which is good, but I would have liked a brother or sister to play with.

If you had magic like Mrs. Eckles, what would you do first?
If I could work magic, I would sort out world peace first, then give myself the ability to fly. Then I'd make my favorite things like cheese, wine, chocolate, and cake really good for you—the more of those you eat, the healthier you get. That'd be good.

What's your favorite type of candy?
My favorite type of candy at the moment is saltwater taffy, which I tried on my recent trip to California. Yum, yum, YUM!

Have you ever been lost? What happened?
I often got lost as a child. I was a bit of a dreamer and wandered off. My mum and dad shouted at me. I regularly get both me and my husband lost on car trips, most recently in California. I am a terrible map reader. What happened? We relied upon kindly folk to point us in the right direction, and my husband tried very hard not to shout at me. I could tell he was fed up, though.

If you could invent one potion, what would it be?

A Kindness Drink. It would be on sale in all the supermarkets. One swig and you would be happy, good natured, and kind to every living thing. No more wars. No more bullying. We could force-feed it to all the meanies who make life nasty. It would taste wonderful, too. Probably of cheese, wine, chocolate, and cake.

What was your first job, and what was your "worst" job?

My first (and worst) job was picking carnations in a greenhouse. It was hot, backbreaking work, and badly paid. The foreman shouted and had hairs growing out of his ears.

How did you celebrate publishing your first book?

I had a baby! Her name is Ella, and she is now twenty-five. My husband arrived at the hospital with the book in his hand, and she arrived shortly afterwards.

Where do you write your books?

In my little blue upstairs office, which has a starry ceiling and lots of fairy lights.

What challenges do you face in the writing process, and how do you overcome them?

I am not too good at planning ahead. My plots sometimes take a wrong turn. When that happens, I leave the story for a while and do something else. Inspiration will come, hopefully. . . .

Which of your characters is most like you?

Wilf and I have a terror of heights in common. We're pretty clumsy, too. But I think we're both helpful and look on the bright side.

What makes you laugh out loud?

People doing funny dancing, or falling down. I'm a sucker for pratfalls.

What do you do on a rainy day?

I read, or write, or curl up in front of the TV and watch comedy.

What's your idea of fun?

A party! I love a dance, me.

What's your favorite song?

Impossible to pick one. I must? Oh, all right. "Song for You," by Leon Russell.

Who is your favorite fictional character?

William Brown in *Just William*, by Richmal Crompton.

What was your favorite book when you were a kid? Do you have a favorite book now?

Just William. Still my favorite.

What's your favorite TV show or movie?

Too many to pick just one. But Disney's *Robin Hood* is up there. The jailhouse scene with the little mice makes me cry every time.

If you were stranded on a desert island, who would you want for company?

My husband and daughter and my two cats, Heathcliff and Jeremy.

If you could travel anywhere in the world, where would you go and what would you do?

I'd go to a remote desert island with a group of favorite friends and family who would come and go. I'd swim with the fishes and eat a lot of barbecue. A speed boat would come every night and ask if anyone wanted to go to a party on the island next door. Sometimes I would. Sometimes I'd have an early night, under the stars. Failing that, Brazil. And the U.S., of course. I'd like to see some real cowboys.

If you could travel in time, where would you go and what would you do?

I have thought a lot about this. I'm torn. I'm curious to see what the future holds, but how great would it be to see what the Tudors really were like. Or the Stone Age. Wow.

What's the best advice you have ever received about writing?

Don't give up. Keep trying. You'll get better. And always write from the heart.

What advice do you wish someone had given you when you were younger?

Send off one of your stories to a publisher. Writing for a living will be more fun than what you're doing now.

Do you ever get writer's block? What do you do to get back on track?

Leave it and move on to another project. Hopefully, my brain will come up with the solution in its own time. I get harder to live with, though. It makes me grumpy and anxious when the ideas won't flow on demand.

What do you want readers to remember about your books?

That they cheered them up.

What would you do if you ever stopped writing?

Read even more, take long, luxurious baths, go on long walks, and think about learning the saxophone.

What should people know about you?

I like cheese, cats, and comedians. I bear grudges. I can be grumpy when dinner's late. I love sleeping.

What do you like best about yourself?
I'm a good friend, I think. I try not to let people down.

Do you have any strange or funny habits?
I watch a lot of rubbish television. I like a fan blowing icy air over me in bed, even in winter.

Did you have funny habits when you were a kid?
I buried things in the garden. Small toys. Plastic brooches. Can't remember why.

What do you consider to be your greatest accomplishment?
My lovely daughter. She did it herself, I suppose, but I tried to be a good mum.

What do you wish you could do better?
Understand technology. I still think my computer is run by a load of invisible elves. It's all beyond me. Luckily, I have a husband who helps me out.

What would your readers be most surprised to learn about you?
I've been published since 1985 and have written over 130 books, but I'm not rich. Not many writers are. I've loved every minute, but I'm not sitting in a castle writing this. Having your name on a book doesn't mean you take exotic holidays and eat lobster every night. But I don't really mind. I do it for love.

GOFISH

questions for the illustrator

JOHANNA WRIGHT

© Gabe Blair

What did you want to be when you grew up?
I really wanted to be a children's book writer and illustrator!

When did you realize you wanted to be an illustrator?
When I was in sixth grade, we made children's books for a school project. Something about it felt so right. I knew I wanted to do that all of the time when I grew up!

What's your most embarrassing childhood memory?
I've always been really grossed out by blood and guts. On my very first day of middle school, in my very first health class, I started to feel woozy when we watched a first aid video. I stood up to excuse myself from the room, and I fainted in front of the whole class!

What's your favorite childhood memory?
I have a lot of nice childhood memories, but I especially loved being at the beach when I was a kid. I would wander around making up stories and playing games in the sand with my brother and sisters.

As a young person, who did you look up to most?

I really looked up to children's book writers (still do). Judy Blume and Beverly Cleary are my greatest heroes.

What was your first job, and what was your "worst" job?

Well, I did a lot of babysitting when I was younger, but my very first job was when I was fifteen and I cleaned dorm rooms in the summer at the University of Oregon. It was pretty fun. We listened to music and joked around a lot. The worst job I ever had? Well, I worked in a nursing home kitchen when I was a teen. The job itself was fine, and the people were great, but we had to be there at four in the morning to start work. It was tough getting up that early!

How did you celebrate publishing your first book?

When I got my first book deal, I was beyond excited. I jumped up and down and ran around the room. My husband and I went out for Thai food. When I actually finished making my first book and sent it off to the publisher, I went to Breitenbush Hot Springs with my husband and family. We stayed in a little cabin in the snow. It was a very peaceful and restful time after a lot of hard work!

Where do you work on your illustrations?

These days, we've turned an upstairs room in our house into my studio. I have a big wooden table that holds all of my paints and brushes, and lots of shelves for my canvas and other art supplies.

Where do you find inspiration for your illustrations?

I'm inspired a lot by my own childhood experiences, and being in nature.

Where do you go for peace and quiet?

I still love to go to the beach, or for a nice walk in the woods, but my very favorite place to sit and think is in a noisy coffee shop!

What makes you laugh out loud?
A lot of things! I love funny stuff. Far Side cartoons still get me every time.

Who is your favorite fictional character?
It would have to be a tie between Ramona Quimby and Anne of Green Gables. Love them both equally, for different reasons!

What are you most afraid of?
Volcanoes! And tidal waves!

If you were stranded on a desert island, who would you want for company?
The Muppets. And my family. And someone incredibly clever at making things, like a radio out of coconuts . . .

If you could travel in time, where would you go and what would you do?
Wow! I would want to go to so many places! For some reason I've always been really fascinated with the early 1900s. I would love to travel to places like New York, Chicago, Portland, Paris, and London in the early 1900s. I would people watch and sketch in a little secret notebook.

What's the best advice you have ever received about illustrating?
Illustrate what you're passionate about, not what you think other people will like.

What do you want readers to remember about your books?
I would love for readers to remember how they felt about my books. I like the idea of pictures and words inspiring feelings and memories in people, and that's what I try to evoke when I create something.

What would you do if you ever stopped illustrating?

Well, that would be sad! But if for some reason I couldn't, or didn't want to anymore, I imagine that I would focus my energy on writing more stories. I love storytelling in all forms, and would find a way to do that!

What do you like best about yourself?

My brain!

What do you consider to be your greatest accomplishment?

I try to keep an open mind and an open heart about life, even when that is painful or hard.

What do you wish you could do better?

Team sports! I've never been very good at things like baseball and soccer.

What would your readers be most surprised to learn about you?

I am easily hypnotized.

What's the strangest dream you've ever had?

I had a really vivid dream a few years ago that the whole world was made out of puffy pillows. Even the ocean was a big cushion that you could bounce on!

What was your favorite thing about school?

Creative projects, reading, writing.

What was your least favorite thing about school?

I had a hard time paying attention in class. I spent a lot of time daydreaming and staring at the floor. I got in trouble for that!

If you could travel anywhere in the world, where would you go and what would you do?

I would love to go anywhere where the ocean is warm, and I would spend all day swimming!

Who is your favorite artist?

I love so many artists, but one of my all-time favorite illustrators is Gyo Fujikawa.

What is your favorite medium to work in?

Acrylic paint on canvas.

What was your favorite book or comic/graphic novel when you were a kid? What's your current favorite?

I actually never read comics as a kid! There are so many good ones out now, but I can't say that I have a favorite.

What were your hobbies as a kid? What are your hobbies now, aside from illustrating?

When I was a kid, I loved drawing and reading, but I also loved to play a game that my sisters and friends and I made up called "little people." We collected scraps of fabric, tiny dolls, and miniature furniture and used those things to build small, elaborate houses on the living room floor. These days, I love being outside, swimming, reading, and writing. And I still love little things . . .

What challenges do you face in the artistic process, and how do you overcome them?

Sometimes in the beginning of a project, everything is a mess and it feels really daunting and scary. What if I can't do it? What if it won't be very good? I've found that it's best to just keep moving forward, and not get bogged down by fear and doubt. It will come together if you just keep going!

Clover Twig works for a Witch, looks for adventure with her clumsy friend Wilf, lives in a magical cottage, and must defend herself from the evil Mesmeranza!

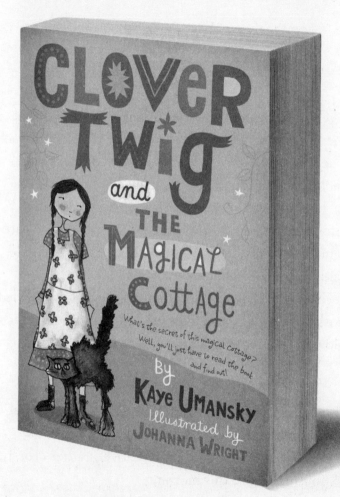

Find out all the witchy secrets in . . .

CLOVER TWIG and THE MAGICAL COttAGE

Chapter One

Wonted.
Storng gril to cleen.

Clover Twig stood at the garden gate, staring in at the Witch's cottage—and the cottage stared right back. The windows were like black eyes—small, dark, and sunken. Ivy drooped over them, like hooded eyelids.

The gate was secured with a loop of old string. Clover pulled it free and gave a brisk push. The gate remained firmly closed. She pushed again. The gate said: "Take the hand off!"

The voice came from deep within the bars. It sounded bossy, like a guard in a museum who has spotted you blowing your nose on a priceless tapestry.

"What?" said Clover.

"Take the hand off!" This time, the order was accompanied by a puff of rust, most of which showered down onto Clover's boots.

"Well, thanks for that," said Clover, rather crossly. "I polished those this morning."

She had, too. She had gone out of her way to look her best. Her old green dress was faded, but clean and well pressed. Her brown cloak was getting to be a bit small for her, but she had let down the hem as far as it would go. Her brown hair was in tidy braids, and her clear blue eyes gazed out from a thoroughly scrubbed face. Altogether neat and respectable, which is how she liked to look.

"The hand. Take it off. Then go away."

Clover kept her hand right where it was. She wasn't about to be ordered around by an old gate, even if it did belong to a Witch.

"I'm not going anywhere," she said, firmly. "And I won't take my hand off until you give me a bit of service. How come you're able to talk, anyway?"

"How should I know? I'm a gate."

"I suppose it's some kind of magic spell, is it?"

"Not my department. I open, I shut. That's it."

Clover glanced up at the watchful windows. Behind one, she thought she saw a movement.

It's her, she thought. She's waiting in the dark behind the curtain. Waiting to see if I'm put off. Well, I'm not.

"Let me in," she said. "I'm here to see Mrs. Eckles."

"Name?" snapped the gate.

"Clover Twig."

"Friend or foe?"

"Friend. But if I was a foe, I'd hardly be likely to say so, would I?"

"Oh ho! Back talking now. That's not going to get you in, is it?"

"What is, then?" Clover was getting tired of standing around arguing with a gate. She gave it another shove.

"Just don't push me," snapped the gate. "Purpose of visit?"

"I'm here about the job." Clover reached into her basket, produced an old envelope, and held it up. "See?"

On the back, in a spidery scrawl blissfully untroubled by punctuation and proper spelling were the following words:

WANTed
STOrNg gRIL To CLEEN aPPLy mRS ECkLES COTTaGE iN THE Wud sicks PenS A wEEK bRiNG AN AYpRUN

Beneath was a small, rudimentary map, consisting of scribbled lines, thumb marks, and a lot of very badly drawn trees. In the middle was what looked like a toddler's attempt at drawing a house together with an arrow and the word ME!

Clover had spotted it the day before, crookedly pinned on the village notice board. It was the six pence that had caught her eye. Six whole pennies! Most cleaning jobs didn't pay more than four pence. It was too good to miss—although she had a feeling that her mother would have something to say.

"Password?" rapped the gate.

"Password?"

"You heard me."

"I don't know anything about a password."

"In that case," sneered the gate with relish, "admittance denied."

Just at that moment, a testy voice shouted: "Is that gate givin' you grief?" It came from behind the front door.

"Yes," called Clover. "It's going on about a password."

"Ah, it's just bein' difficult. Give it a kick."

"With pleasure," said Clover. And she drew back her foot and gave the gate a small, but very hard, kick. It flew open with a furious squeal of hinges.

"Thank you so very much," said Clover, and walked through with her nose in the air. Behind her, there came a huffy crash, which she ignored.

And then she was in the Witch's garden.

It wasn't a pretty sight. Thistles, nettles, and weeds, jostling for space. A collapsed washing line. A crumbling well. An old bucket lying on its side in the mud, trailing a frayed bit of rope. An ancient water barrel, covered with green scum. It didn't bode well.

Clover stared up the path, giving the cottage her full attention. It was old. Very old. The thatch was going bald. The walls were held together by creepers, and the whole structure sagged heavily to one side, as though it was too exhausted to stand up straight.

The cottage still had that watchful air, like it was inspecting her. Giving her the once-over.

Clover didn't even blink. She was good at staring. She wasn't about to lose a staring match with a pile of old bricks. Not after coming all this way.

Finding the cottage had taken forever. It was well off the beaten track, and the map was hopeless. But Clover had a stubborn streak and liked to finish what she started. She came from a large, hopelessly chaotic family. Somebody had to take charge and get things done.

The staring match was getting nowhere, so Clover decided to call it a draw. She thrust the paper into her pocket and walked up to the flaking front door, which unhelpfully lacked a knob, handle, knocker, or bell. She gave a brisk knock.

"I'm here," she called, half-expecting the door to talk back to her.

Silence. Clover waited, straightening a crease in her dress. She would have liked to have worn her better blue one, but it was torn. By Sorrel, of course—the youngest of her three sisters. She coveted Clover's blue dress and was always sneakily trying it on.

Clover rapped again.

"Mrs. Eckles? Are you there?"